William Sloane Kennedy

Oliver Wendell Holmes

Poet, littérateur, scientist

William Sloane Kennedy

Oliver Wendell Holmes
Poet, littérateur, scientist

ISBN/EAN: 9783337419738

Printed in Europe, USA, Canada, Australia, Japan

Cover: Foto ©Raphael Reischuk / pixelio.de

More available books at **www.hansebooks.com**

OLIVER WENDELL HOLMES

POET, LITTÉRATEUR,
SCIENTIST

BY

WILLIAM SLOANE KENNEDY

AUTHOR OF A "LIFE OF HENRY WADSWORTH LONGFELLOW," ETC.

"Two Single Gentlemen roll'd into One."
George Colman, the Younger.

BOSTON

S. E. CASSINO AND COMPANY

1883

" It is an ungenerous silence which leaves all the fair words of honestly-earned praise to the writer of obituary notices and the marble-worker."

OLIVER WENDELL HOLMES.

PREFATORY NOTE.

THE following work does not profess to be a biography in the strictly technical sense (may the proper time for such an undertaking be long deferred!); but it is designed to serve as a treasury of information concerning the ancestry, childhood, college life, professional and literary career, and social surroundings of him of whom it treats, as well as to furnish a careful critical study of his works. I have also added a full bibliography of the writings of Dr. Holmes to date, including his contributions to periodical literature.

W. S. K.

OLD CAMBRIDGE, MASS.,
New Year's Day, 1883.

CONTENTS.

OLIVER WENDELL HOLMES.

OLIVER WENDELL HOLMES.

CHAPTER I.

THE TRIPLE-BRANCHED TREE.

THE twenty-ninth day of August, in the year eighteen hundred and nine, was Commencement Day in a double sense in the town of Cambridge, Massachusetts; for on that day of smiles and greetings, — the merriest of all the year, the day of the graduating festival of Harvard College, — the Rev. Dr. Abiel Holmes entered in his little almanac the memorandum, "Son b.," at the same time sprinkling over the writing a few grains of sand, which still glisten upon the page just as they did when he closed the book, seventy-four years ago.

It was commencement in a double sense, and it was commencement in a triple sense; since, in addition to the beginnings that have already been mentioned, there was in the nerves that feeling of new vigor, in the landscape that touch of garnet and crimson, in the air that tinge of coolness, and in all nature that strange stillness, that kind of dead-point in the revolving wheel of the seasons, which, combined with the chirping of the black-coat crickets, and the first goldening of the golden-rods, formed unmistakable premonitions of the approach of the autumnal season, the pleasantest time of the year in New England. It was under cheerful auspices, then, that the laughing philosopher (at that time, however, the little crying philosopher) of St. Botolph's town took his first degree, and made his first public speech, graduating *summa cum laude* from the dormitory of his *alma mater.* In the country at large, however, there happened to be great depression of spirits and flagging of business interests, owing to the embargo, or non-intercourse policy, enacted and enforced by the American government against the then warring European powers. There was in Boston at that time an almost total cessation of commerce; her merchant ships lay rotting at the wharves, or were drawn up on the beach and dismantled; and the sound of the busy hammer was unheard in her ship-yards. But all this was to be changed in a few years (after the war of 1812) by international adjustment and proclamation of peace.

The ancestral tree of Oliver Wendell Holmes, whose birth we have just been relating, is a triple-branched one, and the three branches are memorized in his own name. By way of sportive symbol, we might hang upon the Oliver branch a loaf of brown bread ("rye 'n' injun") and a pot of baked beans; upon the Wendell branch a doughnut, or Dutch olykoek; and upon the Holmes branch a wooden nutmeg. We will begin with the olykoek branch.

The mother of our poet was Sarah Wendell, daughter of the Hon. Oliver Wendell of Boston. The Wendells are a Dutch family who came to Boston from Albany in the eighteenth century, and it is doubtless largely from them that Dr. Holmes has inherited the solid practical qualities — thrift, industry, caution, — which have made him successful as a physician and professor. Perhaps his humor, too, came in with that Dutch strain of blood. In his poem on "The Hudson" the Autocrat says that his mother used often to sing in soft lullaby the story of his descent from the Albany Wendells :—

"'There flows a fair stream by the hills of the
    West,' —
She sang to her boy as he lay on her breast;
'Along its smooth margin thy fathers have
    played;
Beside its deep waters their ashes are laid.'"

The original settler in Albany was Evert Jansen Wendell, who, about the year 1645, came from Embden, in East Friesland, a town just on the border-line between Germany and the Netherlands. We know that in 1656 Evert was the *Regerendo Dijaken* of the Dutch church in Albany, but details of the lives of the early ancestors are very scarce.* Other early members of the church were Evert Wendell, his wife Merritje, and his sons John and Evert. Two of the family

---

* To get an idea of Dutch life in America one should study Irving's "Knickerbocker" (with caution and abatements), as well as the numerous early annals of New York and Albany.

were shoemakers ; some were fur-traders ; and the family is still a wealthy and powerful one in Albany. The old square Dutch church (1715–1806) was extremely quaint, resembling a good deal, one would judge, the present Swedes' church in Philadelphia. The walls were perforated near the top with loop-holes, and when there was danger of an invasion the stout burghers sat through the service with their guns beside them, smoking their pipes and wearing their hats and muffs. The stoves were placed on posts in the air, and were against and on a level with the galleries. The hats of the men were ordinarily hung on rows of nails placed along the front of the galleries. There was an hour-glass on the pulpit for the guidance of the preacher. The window-panes were five inches square, and upon them were emblazoned the names and family arms of some of the church-members. The arms of the Wendells (a ship riding at two anchors) were stained on some panes of the east window.* Other quaint mansions

---

* It is a pity that none of these old stained window-panes survive. The arms of the Wendells are, however, given in Thomas Bridgman's " Memorials of the

of the old patrons, or Knickerbackers, were the Koeymans' mansion, the houses of the Verplancks, and the residence of the fur-trader, Harman Wendell, a cut of which is given in *Harper's Monthly Magazine* for April, 1857.*   (See also "Collections of the History of Albany.")

It would need a Van Ostade or a Teniers to paint the domestic life of these high-stomached, home-loving, portly old Hollanders of Albany, — these old Walter the Doubters, and Peter the Headstrongs, sitting by their firesides with their pipes, and pondering their unutterable ponderings. But come, Mr. Artist, you can at least paint us, if you please, the typical Dutch mansion, with its low-sweeping eaves, glazed windows, tiled roof, and gable of small, imported black and yellow bricks, the narrow windows, the grotesque face of the well-burnished knocker, the date of erection in figures of iron on the door, and the absurd

Dead in Boston" (King's Chapel Burying Ground), Boston, 1853.

* A good example of a reproduction of the general features of the antique Dutch gable of these old Albany houses may be seen in the brick residence built a few years ago by Mr. F. B. Sanborn, of Concord, Mass.

painted weather-cock on the roof. And paint us, too, the well-scrubbed sto*e*p, the sanded floors, the spare-room hung round with many-colored petticoats, the huge kitchen with its flaming side-board, its festoons of dried apples and ears of Indian corn, the fireplace, the tea-table with its elephantine delftware tea-pot (richly painted), its great dish of brown pork-scraps, huge apple-pie, and dish of olykoeks. And, finally, let us see at her household tasks the good wife, with her neatly-braided hair and high-heeled shoes; and by the fireside show us the worthy burgomaster with his homespun coat, his ten or twenty (or such a matter) pairs of breeches, his huge shoe-buckles, eel-skin queue, broad-brimmed hat, and long, painted, delftware pipe. Some such picture as this (only somewhat toned down) we should have to present to our minds if we would know how the early Wendells lived.

Two of the Albany Dutchmen — the brothers, Abraham and Jacob — came to Boston early in the eighteenth century, as has been stated. Of these, Jacob was the great-grandfather of Oliver Wendell Holmes. He was one of the wealthiest merchants of Boston, was colonel of the Boston regiment, and member of the city council, resided in a brick mansion on the southwest corner of Tremont and School Streets. He married Sarah, daughter of Dr. James Oliver. Tradition says that Jacob caught his first glimpse of his future wife as he was one day passing by her father's house, and when she was only nine years old; and that he was so much struck with her beauty that he purposed then and there in his heart to wait for her to grow up that he might make her his wife. Jacob had twelve children who married into the Oliver, the Sewall, and the Phillips families. The youngest daughter married William Phillips, the first mayor of Boston, whose son, Wendell Phillips, has rendered the name familiar to the present generation.* The distant relationship between Wendell Phillips and Oliver Wendell Holmes was humorously alluded to by the poet in his "Post-Prandial," Phi Beta Kappa poem of 1881 :—

" Fair cousin Wendell P.,
Our ancestors were dwellers beside the Zuyder Zee;
Both Grotius and Erasmus were countrymen of we,
And Vondel was our namesake, though he spelt it with
    a V."

* Heraldic Journal, April, 1865

Jacob Wendell died in 1761. His son Oliver (the grandfather of Dr. Holmes), born in 1733, and graduated at Harvard College in 1753, entered into the mercantile business with his father in Boston. He became Judge of Probate for Suffolk County, was a member of the Corporation of Harvard College from 1778 to 1812, was a selectman during the siege of Boston, and joined in the congratulatory address to Washington upon its termination; he was, moreover, employed by Major-General Greene, upon an order of Washington, to procure men to watch the British by land and sea after the evacuation, in order that no spies might convey intelligence to the British commanders of the movements of the American troops. (See Drake's "Old Landmarks of Boston," pp. 65, 66). Judge Wendell married Mary, daughter of Edward and Dorothy (Quincy) Jackson. The judge's daughter Sarah married the Rev. Abiel Holmes, and became the mother of Oliver Wendell Holmes. Judge Wendell passed his last years in quiet retirement in the old Holmes mansion in Cambridge. In the latter part of his life he was burdened with lameness and other infirmities of age. He died in 1818 at the age of eighty-four, bequeathing the Holmes estate to his daughter.   He was distinguished, says his friend, President Quincy, for uncommon urbanity of manners, and unimpeachable integrity of conduct.   The punctuality with which he performed the duties of office were highly exemplary.

We shall now say good-by to the worthy Wendell burghers, and pay our respects to the brown loaf (or Boston) branch of Dr. Holmes' ancestral tree.

The Dorothy Quincy, who was the wife of Edward Jackson, and the mother-in-law of Judge Oliver Wendell, is the great-grandmother of the poet, and is the one whose portrait is celebrated by him in his well-known poem, "Dorothy Q." : —

> " Hold up the canvas full in view, —
>   Look ! there's a rent the light shines through,
>   Dark with a century's fringe of dust, —
>   That was a Red-Coat's rapier-thrust !
>   Such is the tale the lady old,
>   Dorothy's daughter's daughter told."

The first Quincy was Edmund. He was

one of the first settlers of Boston, and lived in Wollaston, now Quincy. It is unnecessary to do more than refer to the members of this family, whose name and works are familiar to all students of American history. The first Josiah Quincy, distinguished as a patriot, died young and greatly lamented; the second of that name, statesman and scholar, President of Harvard University, and author of a history of that institution, was one of the first to denounce the slaveholding tyranny in America; the third of the same name, ex-mayor of Boston, has long been identified with the municipal interests of the city. The estate of the family was on the site of the present Quincy Block. The house was a stately pilastered structure, with honey-suckles and high damask rose-bushes twining about its porch, — its lawn a glacis adorned with tall robin-and-oriole-haunted elms. There were three Dorothy Quincys in the family. The Dorothy who was the niece of Dr. Holmes' great-grandmother was the wife of John Hancock, one of the signers of the Declaration of Independence. She was a noble, strong-willed woman of the old heroic

type.   It is related of her that at one period
of her life she was accustomed to invite all
classes to her Saturday salt-fish dinners at
the well-known mansion fronting Boston
Common.   On one occasion, when Admiral
d'Estaing and his three hundred officers had
been invited to breakfast with Mr. Hancock,
and sufficient milk could not be procured,
she sent out her servants with orders to milk
sans cérémonie all the cows they could find on
the Common, and to send to her any one who
complained.   It is said that the owners of
the cows took the jest in the best of humor,
laughing heartily at her free and unconventional procedure.*

* For the genealogy of the Quincys, see the " New
England Historical and Genealogical Register" for
1857, p. 2.   In the same journal for 1881, p. 39, a
writer gets his " Dorothy Q.'s" pretty badly mixed. And
the subject is still further confused in the minds of
others. At a breakfast given to Dr. Holmes, in 1879, by
the Rev. Dr. Henry C. Potter, in the rooms of the
Century Club, New York, Chief Justice Daly is reported by a newspaper to have made the following neat
repartee apropos of " Dorothy Q.": —

" ' I was present' (Judge Daly is speaking) ' last
Thursday evening when Mr. Holmes read to a highly-
gratified circle several of his poems, with an account of
how they came to be written. The one that especially

To turn now to the Olivers. This strain of blood came in with Jacob Wendell, who married Sarah Oliver, daughter of Dr. James Oliver. The first Oliver was Thomas, who came to Boston from London in 1632. Daniel Oliver, father of Lieutenant-Governor Andrew Oliver, was for many years a councillor in Boston, and died in 1732. His will contained the following provision:—

"*Imprimis*, I give and bequeath my house adjoining to Barton's Rope-Walk, called Spinning House, with the lands as now fenced

fixed my attention was " Dorothy Q.," especially when he informed us that that lady was his great-grandmother.'

" *Mr. Holmes.* — ' My grandmother, Judge ?' "

" *Judge Daly.* — ' I apologize to your grandmother for depriving her memory of the nearer share she had in your creation. ' "

Now, unfortunately for this reported repartee, the poem itself shows (if the genealogies did not do so) that " Dorothy Q. " was the great-grandmother of the poet. The opening words of the poem tell us that the verses are about " grandmother's mother," and in the second stanza it is written,

> " Such is the tale the lady old,
> *Dorothy's daughter's daughter told.*"

The " daughter's daughter " here refers to Dr. Holmes' mother.

in, — about fifty feet square, — with all the
profits and incomes of it, as it now stands in
my books (since built), forever to be improved
for learning poor children of the town of Boston to read the word of God, and to write, if
need be, or any other work of charity for the
public good." (Mem. Hist. Boston, II. 539,
note.)

Lieutenant-Governor Andrew Oliver, the
obnoxious stamp distributor who was burned
in effigy, was one of the most affluent of the
old Bostonians, and had a private establishment equal to that of any in the province.
Coaches, chariot, negro slaves, and good
sterling plate in abundance bore witness to
his wealth.

In his paper on "The Medical Profession
in Massachusetts," published in a volume of
Lowell Institute Lectures, by the Massachusetts Historical Society, in 1869, Dr. Holmes
has a few characteristic remarks about his
great-great-grandfather, Dr. James Oliver,
who died in 1703. He says: "When I was
yet of trivial age, and suffered occasionally,
as many children do, from what one of my
Cambridgeport schoolmates used to call

'ager,' — meaning thereby toothache, or faceache, — I used to get relief from a certain plaster which never went by any other name than 'Dr. Oliver.'" Dr. Oliver practised in Cambridge, and his descendant found among some old books a small manuscript account-book of his, by which it appears that other remedies used by him in that day were the usual simples, elder, parsley, fennel, saffron, snake-root, and the Elixir Proprietatis, with other elixirs and cordials, as if he rather fancied warming medicines. One of the items in the account-book is a bill against the estate of Samuel Pason, of Roxbury, for services rendered during his last illness. Says Dr. Holmes, "It is a source of honest pride to his descendant that his bill, which was honestly paid, as it seems to have been honorably earned, amounted to the handsome sum of seven pounds and two shillings. Let me add that he repeatedly prescribes plasters, one of which was very probably the 'Dr. Oliver' that soothed my infant griefs, and for which, I blush to say, that my venerated ancestor received from Goodman Hancock the painfully exiguous sum of no pounds, no shillings, and sixpence." *

We come now to the Bradstreets. Sarah Oliver (wife of Jacob Wendell) was the daughter of Mercy Bradstreet, who was the daughter of Dr. Samuel Bradstreet, son of Governor Simon Bradstreet and Anne Dudley. Simon Bradstreet was Governor of the Massachusetts Colony in 1689. He was educated at Emanuel College, Cambridge, and came to America with Winthrop. The Labadist missionaries † described him as an old man, quiet and grave, dressed in black silk, but not sumptuously. The arms of the Bradstreets are impressed on the seal attached to Governor Bradstreet's will, which is on file at the Suffolk Probate Office in Boston. The crest is also found on a piece of embroidery preserved in the family. Burke gives the arms of one of the English Bradstreets as follows, and they are substantially those of Governor Bradstreet : —

Ar. a greyhound, pas. gu., on a chief, sa., three crescents or.

* For the Oliver Genealogy, see " New England Historical and Genealogical Register," 1865, p. 101.

† See Long Island Hist. Soc. Coll., I.

Mrs. Anne Dudley Bradstreet was, as is well known to students of American literature, the first poet of the New World, — her book, "The Tenth Muse lately sprung up in America" (London, 1650), being the first volume of original verse by an American. She was the daughter of Governor Thomas Dudley, to whom Mather applies this epitaph : —

> " In books a prodigal they say ;
> A living cyclopædia ;
> Of histories of church and priest,
> A full compendium, at least ;
> A table-talker, rich in sense,
> And witty without wit's pretence."

Mrs. Bradstreet's poems went through eight editions. The Harvard College library possesses a copy (presented by James Russell Lowell) of the small-sized second edition. It is a pretty damaged article of book, and seems to have been in its day a *vade-mecum* of various lovers of poesy. Readers of this day, however, will scarcely welter in delight over it, as President John Rogers of Harvard College said he did. In that day, the fact of a woman being able to write anything of merit was regarded as almost miraculous, and excited in some quarters adverse criticism. Ward, author of the " Simple Cobbler," in his adulatory verses prefixed to Mrs. Bradstreet's poems, puts this sentiment into the mouth of Apollo : —

> " It half revives my chil frost-bitten blood,
> To see a Woman once, do aught that's good."

The title of her book will indicate the nature of its contents : " Several Poems compiled with great variety of Wit and Learning, full of Delight ; Wherein especially is contained a compleat Discourse, and Description of the Four Elements, Constitutions, Ages of Man, Seasons of the Year, together with an exact Epitome of the three first Monarchyes, viz., The Assyrian, Persian, Grecian, And beginning of the Romane Commonweal to the end of their last King : With diverse other pleasant and serious Poems. By a Gentlewoman in New-England. The second Edition, Corrected by the Author, and enlarged by an Addition of several Poems found amongst her Papers after her Death. Boston, Printed by John Foster, 1678."

There are a few enjoyable passages in the poems. In the piece on " Summer " we read, —

" Now go those frolick Swains, the Shepherd Lads
To wash the thick cloth'd flocks with pipes full
     glad,
In the cool streams they labor with delight,
Rubbing their dirty coats till they look white.

   .   .   .   .   .

" This moneth the Roses are distil'd in glasses,
Whose fragrant smel all made perfumes surpasses,
The Cherry, Gooseberry are now in th' prime,
And for all sorts of Pease, this is the time.

   .   .   .   .   .

" I heard the merry grasshopper then sing,
The black clad Cricket, bear a second part,
They kept one tune, and plaid on the same string,
Seeming to glory in their little Art."

In the Epilogue, entitled " The Author to her Book," she says : —

" Thou ill-form'd offspring of my feeble brain,
Who after birth did'st by my side remain,
Till snatcht from thence by friends, less wise than
     true,
Who thee abroad, expos'd to publick view,

Made thee in raggs, halting to th' press to trudg,
Where errors were not lessened (all may judg).
At thy return my blushing was not small
My rambling brat (in print) should mother call,
I cast thee by as one unfit for light,
Thy Visage was so irksome in my sight ;
Yet being mine own, at length affection would
Thy blemishes amend, if so I could," etc.

Among the descendants of Mrs. Bradstreet we may enumerate, besides the poet Holmes, Dr. William Ellery Channing, the Rev. Joseph Buckminster Lee, the two Richard Henry Danas, and Wendell Phillips. Mrs. Bradstreet's complete works have been sumptuously edited in a single quarto volume by John Harvard Ellis (Charlestown: Abram E. Cutter, 1867).

Let us now turn our attention to the Holmes family, which we have jestingly styled the wooden-nutmeg branch, the original seat of the family being at Woodstock, called the best and fairest of all the agricultural towns of Connecticut. Lower, in his "English Surnames" (3d ed. vol. i., p. 74), says that the surname Holm, or Holmes, is classed among those local names which describe the nature or situation of the original bearer's residence, such as Hill, Dale, Wood. He defines it as follows : "Holm, Holmes, flat land, a meadow surrounded with water."

In E. Holmes Bugbee's "Genealogy of the Holmes Family of Woodstock" (Killingly, Conn., 1877; printed on the type-writer), interesting details relating to the various ancestors are given. The first Holmes of this branch of the family was Thomas Holmes of London, a lawyer of Gray's Inn, who was killed during the Civil War at the siege of Oxford (1646). It seems that Woodstock was settled in 1686 by a colony from Roxbury, Mass., and that John Holmes was one of the colony and one of the first proprietors in the new town. John was born about the year 1664, near Boston, and married Hannah, daughter of Isaac Newell, of Roxbury, Mass. He was a prominent man in the new colony and was elected to many important positions in the town. Frequent grants of land were made to him for services rendered to the settlement. His son David, called "Deacon David," was a prominent man in the First Church of Woodstock. His widow Bathsheba (maiden surname unknown) married as her second husband Joseph Edmunds. (By her first husband she had a son David, who became the father of Abiel Holmes, who in turn was the father of Oliver Wendell Holmes, the poet.) Grandmother Edmunds, as she was called by her descendants, lived to an advanced age, and was always spoken of by them as "a remarkable woman, and of recognized authority in all matters of housewifery." She had a wide reputation as a doctress and midwife. It is recorded of her that at the time of the great snow-storm of 1717, when the snow almost buried the houses, she got out of the upper window of her residence in Woodstock, and travelled on snow-shoes over hill and dale to Dudley, Mass., to attend a sick woman. She was accompanied by two men who had hold of the ends of a long pole, she holding on by the middle thereof. The genealogist records the following tradition of this same brave ancestress of our poet:—

"During the Indian troubles in the early part of the eighteenth century there was considerable alarm in all the isolated settlements, and garrison-houses, or forts, were erected, in

which to place the women and children while
the men were away at work in the fields.
On one of these occasions of general alarm,
when the women and children were alone in
the fort, it was proposed that some one of
their number should go to the garden, which
was some way off, and gather vegetables for
dinner. Volunteers were called for, and of
them all in the fort that day Bathsheba
Holmes alone dared to go. Nothing daunted
at the thought that Indians might be lurking
about, — and they were frequently seen, —
she bravely sallied forth, and with her capa-
cious basket wended her way through a long,
narrow, winding path to the garden, and there
gathered of beans and various vegetables a
heaped basketful, and safely returned to the
garrison, where the viands, fresh grown on
virgin soil, and fit food for royal tables, were
skilfully cooked and eaten with thankful
hearts. Many years afterward, — the Indians
almost all gone to other hunting-grounds, and
grandmother Edmunds now an old woman, —
a solitary Indian, decrepit and broken in
spirit, called at her door begging, as was ever
the custom of the red men, for cider, promis-

ing a story if the favor were granted. The
cider was drawn and proffered and the story
told. It was this : On asking her if she remembered going to the garden. with her
basket long years ago, when the women and
children were alone in the fort, and on being
answered in the affirmative, he said he saw
her when she left the fort, and determined
to have her life before she returned. He
secreted himself in the thick brushwood by
the side of the path she would travel, and
when she had approached sufficiently near,
he stoutly bent his bow, and was about to let
the well-aimed arrow fly, when suddenly a
mysterious power forbade him, and stayed his
arm. When she had gone he upbraided himself for being a cowardly Indian, and redeter-
mined to have her life when she returned.
But the same power stayed his arm again,
and he went his way wondering greatly at his
inability to kill a squaw. All the years since
then, he said, he had been watching her as
one who was under the protecting care of
the Indians' God. He thought it was the
Great Spirit that held his arm and saved
her life."

Well for us that Indian's superstition! for if that arrow had been sped it is probable that the world would have had no Oliver Wendell Holmes.

David (2) the paternal grandfather of our poet, married for his first wife Mehitable, daughter of Ephraim Mayhew ; his second wife was Mrs. Temperance Bishop, by whom he had Abiel Holmes. David served in the French and Indian wars as Captain of Colonel Fitch's regiment, through three campaigns — the last terminating with the conquest of Canada. On the first intelligence of the battle of Lexington he joined the army in his professional character of surgeon, and continued in the service till the fourth year of the war, when, worn out with the fatigues of the camp, he returned home, and soon after died, March 19, 1779. Besides Abiel, David had seven other children, brothers and sisters ; one of them (named Lathrop) who was, like his father, a physician, went to Midway, Georgia, and married there, but perished by shipwreck with his wife on the return voyage.

In his poem, "A Family Record," read, in 1877, at the Fourth of July Celebration in

Roseland Park, Woodstock, Dr. Holmes thus alludes to a visit made by him to the home of his ancestors : —

" In days gone by I sought the hallowed ground ;
Climbed yon long slope ; the sacred spot I found
Where all unsullied lies the winter snow,
Where all ungathered Spring's pale violets blow,
And tracked from stone to stone the Saxon name
That marks the blood I need not blush to claim, —
Blood such as warmed the Pilgrim sons of toil,
Who held from God the charter of the soil."

There is a large Holmes family at East Haddam, Conn., but it is not connected with the Woodstock family by any known link in this country. In sly satire upon the folly of American coat-of-arms hunters, Mr. D. Williams Patterson, in his sumptuously printed genealogy of the East Haddam family, offers as a substitute for the ordinary European imitation a bit of Yankee Heraldry, or kind of Indian totemism, in the shape of the following mark of a certain John Holmes (the mark recorded in the Proprietors' book of the town) : "john holmes his marke for his Creturs is two slits one ye top of ye off eare and a half peny one yᵉ under side of yᵉ neare eare. Apriell yᵉ 17th 1716." Mr. Patterson also gives a representation, or cut, which he offers as a substitute for the usual emblazonments of the heraldry books. His "representation" consists of a very creditable picture of the head of a belled heifer with her ears cropped. There is good grim humor about this Patterson. How Carlyle or Thoreau would have liked to expatiate on the sincerity, the eternal veracity, etc., of the heifer's-head coat-of-arms! One is reminded of Sydney Smith, who said that his ancestors never had any arms, and invariably sealed their letters with their thumbs.

We have now swept the wide circuit of the genealogical outskirts of our subject, and are nearly ready to enter the charmed circle of the poet's boyhood, described by himself with such tender and lingering fondness in so many parts of his writings. But first we must present a picture of his father, Abiel Holmes.

Born in Woodstock in 1763, his father David, the surgeon-physician, sent him in 1779, at the age of sixteen, to Yale College.

We are told that young Abiel rode all the way to New Haven on horseback. At college he was considered one of the most accomplished scholars of his class.*

He graduated in 1783; was for a time tutor in the college under President Ezra Stiles; preached for some years in Midway, Georgia; in 1790 married Mary, daughter of President Stiles; in 1791 removed to Cambridge for his health; was installed as pastor of the First Congregational Church in that town (then having about two thousand inhabitants), and remained pastor of the church for forty years. In 1795 his wife died, leaving no children. In 1800 he married Sarah Wendell, by whom he had five children, namely: *Mary Jackson*, born in 1802, married Dr. Usher Parsons, of Providence; *Ann Susan*, born in 1804, married Charles W. Upham, who was successively a clergyman, mayor of Salem, State Senator, and Congressman; *Sarah Lathrop*, born in 1805, died in 1812; *Oliver Wendell*, born

---

* Many of the details immediately following are taken from the eighth volume of the Mass. Hist. Soc. Collections, and from Dr. Alex. McKenzie's Lectures on the History of the First Church in Cambridge.

August 29, 1809; *John*, born 1812. Sarah (Wendell) Holmes, the mother of these children, died August 19, 1862, in the ninety-third year of her age. She was a bright, keen-witted, vivacious woman, much beloved by her neighbors and by her husband's parishioners. Her son, the poet, has dedicated to her one of his books.

In 1807 Dr. Abiel Holmes moved into the famous Gambrel-Roofed House near the College; in 1817 he delivered a course of lectures on Ecclesiastical History in Harvard College; in 1831 he asked a release from his pastoral duties, which was granted, with noble testimonials to his character and learning. He died June 12, 1837, at the age of seventy-four.

The words which Dr. O. W. Holmes applies to the Rev. Pitt Clarke, father of Dr. Edward Hammond Clarke, of Boston, may be used of his own father: "He was one of those excellent New England clergymen whose blood seems to carry the scholarly and personal virtues with it to their descendants, oftentimes for successive generations." He was pre-eminently a scholar and antiquarian, and loved to buy rare old editions of classic works. His contributions to the Massachusetts Historical Society are very numerous, and he was for more than twenty years its corresponding secretary; his handwriting was nearly as plain as print. It was he who, in 1816, discovered in the Prince Library the third manuscript volume of the invaluable Winthrop Journals, which was deciphered and published. Dr. O. W. Holmes once remarked to the writer that he thought his father should have been an historian and antiquarian solely; he said that he himself inherited from him a love of books and an antiquarian taste — a thing that his readers do not need to be told. During the conversation just alluded to Dr. Holmes remarked that it was a curious fact that years before Tennyson made the " In Memoriam " stanza famous, his own father had written verses in that style, which were published by the Stiles family in their " Family Tablet."

The personal appearance of Abiel Holmes was most genial and pleasant, as indeed his portrait, preserved in the rooms of the Massachusetts Historical Society, witnesses. This small oil-portrait shows a symmetrical, massive head, reminding one a good deal of the son's, especially in the unusual height of the cerebral portion, or the part above the ears. The lips are full, showing a rich nature; the nose ample, the face possessing in general a good deal of feature; the expression somewhat professionally clerical, but very kindly and sweet. The artist has painted the good doctor in his surplice and gown, and, although not yet old, he shows signs, as to his head, that he may yet reach the "hairless and cappy" condition. There are those living in Cambridge who remember his pleasant and kindly manners, and tell how as he walked the streets he would often stop to talk with little children, and make them presents of confectionery.

At the Holmes Breakfast in 1879 Colonel T. W. Higginson spoke of him as that most delightful of sunny old men. Colonel Higginson passed his boyhood in Cambridge in a roomy old mansion, which was at that time the very next door to the Gambrel-Roofed House. He relates that one evening when he and some other boys at the house were playing in the library the gray-haired, gentle old divine, who had been taking an interest in their sports,— never complaining of their loudest noise,— went to the frost-covered window, and sketched with his penknife what seemed a clump of bushes and a galaxy of glittering stars, and above it he wrote the inscription, *Per aspera ad astra,* — through difficulties to the stars, —at the same time explaining to the boys what the words meant.

Of a sermon preached by Abiel Holmes, and afterwards printed, a contemporary said : "It reads as placid as he looked: . . . it is another instance of that now lost art of felicitously weaving in Scripture language with the texture of every sentence and the expression of every thought, which gave such peculiar unction to the most common utterances of the elder divines."

The severe Calvinistic faith in which he was bred did not chill his genial social nature. Nor was he in any respect bigoted. His position at Cambridge was a peculiarly delicate one, the Unitarian faith prevailing in the University, and the Unitarian spirit being very strong in the whole community. But his charitable and liberal nature led him to fraternize cordially with all good men, and for years he was in the habit of exchanging pulpits with the Unitarian clergymen of Cambridge and Boston.

Dr. Holmes was one of the founders of the Society for promoting Christian Knowledge, and also of the American Education Society. He was a member of the American Academy of Arts and Sciences, Overseer of Harvard University, and a trustee of the Institution at Andover. He received in 1805 the degree of Doctor of Divinity from the University of Edinburgh, and was made LL.D. by Alleghany College in 1822. In 1801 he published a "History of Cambridge"—a sort of handbook of the town. His life of President Ezra Stiles is clear, lucid, and manly in style, and is excellent reading to this day. Take, for example, this description of the personal appearance and habits of the subject of his memoir:—

"President Stiles was a man of low and small stature; of a very delicate structure; and of a well-proportioned form. His eyes were of a dark gray color; and, in the

moment of contemplation, singularly penetrating. His voice was clear and energetic.
His countenance, especially in conversation,
was expressive of mildness and benignity;
but, if occasion required, it became the index
of majesty and authority. . . .

" He always carried a pencil in his pocket,
and a small quarto sheet of blank paper,
doubled lengthwise, on which he minuted
every noticeable occurrence and useful information. When he travelled he carried several
blank sheets, folded in the same manner, and
applied them to the same purpose. When
these memoranda formed materials sufficient
for a volume he had them bound; and they,
collectively, compose four curious volumes of
Itineraries, preserved in his cabinet of manu-
scripts." *

* At the rooms of the Rhode Island Historical
Society in Providence they show you a little vest-
pocket almanac and note-book of President Stiles, some
of the memoranda in which are in English and some
in Hebrew characters. One of the entries consists of
the following quaint and pithy line: "Col. Ethan
Allen of Vermont died and went to Hell this day!"
Whole volumes of divinity could not better embody the
spirit of Connecticut Puritanism, — as it was and as it
is.

Jared Sparks spoke of Dr. Holmes' American Annals as among the most valuable productions of the American press. It is a book that fetches a high price to this day.

CHAPTER II.

CAMBRIDGE.

TOPOGRAPHICALLY speaking, the city of
Cambridge at the present day is like a vast
spider's web with nine main radii, compacted
with numerous circular and cross lines, along
which, as well as along the chief radii, the
houses are strung like beads of dew.   At the
centre of the web stands the old Gambrel-
Roofed House, and close by are the buildings
of Harvard University; on the south of the
city glides the silent Charles River through
its salt marshes, —

" Full without noise, and whispers in his reeds."

Over all the houses, the old gardens, the aca-
demic quiet, the culture, soars the gargoyled
tower of Memorial Hall, seen from far off as
the most conspicuous feature in the landscape.
There is a particular charm in the rural en-

virons of Cambridge, — its invigorating air, charged full of ozone, iodine, oxygen, its wide prospects, and its beautiful surburban villas. The Belmont and Arlington region is especially beautiful; the hills thrown up against the sky like an embroidered curtain, netted with old winding lanes, and dreamy at dusk with dim indigo and violet tints; at sunset enormous spokes diverging from the sunken orb through gold-smoke and rift and cumulus cloud; in the summer the trees of greenest emerald; in autumn chromatized with red and yellow; the ash trees a cool and delicate purple; the oaks and birches by the pond sides glowing with a subdued glory (garnet and pale lemon) ; and in sequestered woodland walks no sound to break the silence save the rustle of the footsteps through thick rugs of colored leaves. It was impossible that leafy, blossoming old Cambridge, with her population of literary people, should not produce poets. She has had not only three or four eminent bards, but a great many minor ones, as well as a goodly number of writers of poetical prose. Cambridge society is distinguished for a temperate elegance and refinement of life somehow reconciled and harmonized with a most plentiful lack of money. United with the quiet urbanity and reserve which always accompany the finer nervous organizations, there is also the cosmopolitanism of culture and travel, and the timidity of scholarly conservatism ; in religion the polite silence of minds cheerfully resigned to philosophical nescience ; in political matters a subdued cynicism, capable of bursting forth, however, into the fiercest patriotism when stung into activity ; and finally, in the matter of family traditions and caste, a pretty generous democratic indifference, — intellect, personal bravery, and choice manners opening every door, except in the case of a very few idiotic old families. As a matter of course, there are in Cambridge, as in every other college town, two other classes besides that which gives the town its distinctive social complexion, — namely, the tradespeople and the transient student class. Each of these groups keeps up an independent life. Topographically viewed, the arrangement is like that of the Chinese ivory thimble; the first compartment, ring, or layer on the outside is that of "the people," monotonously commonplace and alike in every city, and only in spots original and picturesque ; drawing the circle still closer, you include the old families and the professors' families (culture, pride, limited incomes, charming society, comfortable residences, with here and there a quaint heavy-beamed, ancestral house, occupied by nice old-fashioned people, as snugly ensconced for life with their books and flowers as your heart could wish); and, finally, in the centre comes the student-class with its Bohemian life apart, and glad to be apart.

At the time our poet was born the city had a population of three thousand five hundred souls. Listen to a description of some of its local grandeurs, taken from Dr. Abiel Holmes' "History of Cambridge." He says that " West Boston Bridge, connecting Cambridge with Boston, is a magnificent structure " ! — " There are five (!) college edifices belonging to Harvard University." — " The gardens of Thomas Brattle are universally admired." — " It is generally conceded that this town eminently combines the tranquillity of philosophic solitude with the choicest pleasures and advantages of refined society." That last sentence is as true to-day as it was nearly a hundred years ago ; but how changed is almost everything else ! Cambridge has now some fifty-eight thousand inhabitants, a quarter of a hundred college buildings ; and the gardens of Thomas Brattle, where are they ?

Of the appearance of Cambridge in the early part of this century Lowell has something to say in his delightful "Fireside Travels." He tells of the noisy belfry of the college, the square, brown tower of the little Episcopal church (still in existence), the slim, yellow spire of the parish meeting-house, the few old houses that stood around the bare Common, the half-dozen stately old Georgian houses fronting southward on the "Old Road," — now Mt. Auburn Street, — along which the Charles slipped quietly through green and purple salt-meadows darkened in patches with the "blossoming black grass."

Then there was the snowy-gleaming, vine-covered cottage of the old whitewasher, who had bestowed the candent baptism of his lime upon his house, the stems of his trees, and his fence, and would tolerate, we are told, only whitest fowls and whitest china-asters in his dooryard. There was but one brewer in the town, a certain venerable Ethiopian named Lewis, who manufactured the village beer, both spruce and ginger. His whole stock he carried in a roofed hand-cart, "on whose front a sign-board presented at either end an insurrectionary bottle." The barber's-shop was a sunny little room fronting on the common, — the proverbial loquacity of the place made still more lively by the sweet jangle of birds — canaries, Java sparrows, robin, thrush, and bobolink, and a white cockatoo that, as the barber averred, spoke in the Hottentot language.

The home of a poet's childhood, if a pleasant one, is to him always the most beautiful and poetical spot on earth. There he first dreamed those unutterable dreams of an ideal realm ; there life unfolded its rosy petals noiselessly around his wondering mind, and the crumbling maroon and red-gold cloud-bars of dawn hung trembling over an enchanted land of dreams. How keen the senses ! — that first sniff of fresh cracker-fragrance in a baker's shop ; the scent of that jessamine that clung by grandmother's window; those bees in the gigantic, sunshine-drunken, red hollyhocks; those wonderful great horses in the barn, and those gliding, epicurean old loafers — the frogs in the pond, — but once in our life are we permitted such enjoyment as we took in these things, and that is in the period of childhood, when the universe stretches in soft illusion about us, infinite in mystery and infinite in poetical beauty.

None more fortunate in his childhood than our young Oliver, and no wonder that he has never tired of talking and writing about it.

For a poet to have lived until adolescence in the soothing scholastic quiet of a quaint rural town is something enviable. But if, in addition, he chance to be the son of one of the most influential and beloved citizens of the place, connected with the noblest families in the community, and living in a spacious old mansion consecrated by historical memories, and surrounded by flowers and trees and gardens — breathed over twice a day by the sweet breath of the sea, — then we may count his childhood as almost an ideally perfect one. And such a happiness as this fell to the

lot of Oliver Wendell Holmes. The old
yellow hip-roofed house in which he was born
is now, alas! fairly over-crowed and out-
shone by the two large and elegant buildings
erected immediately at its side and rear,
namely, the Harvard College Gymnasium (of
brick) and the new brown-stone Law School
Building. The old house now seems to wear
almost a shamefaced look, like an old lady
in mits and calash bonnet in the midst of an
audience of fashionable young people. In
Dr. Holmes' youth there stood in the immediate neighborhood of the old manse the Red
Lion Tavern, the quaint barber-shop described
by Lowell in his " Fireside Travels," and the
house of Royal Morse, of college fame, resi-
dent here from 1809 to 1872. Somewhere
about the place there was a honeysuckle
vine, with its pink and white perfumed
blossoms, and on the western side of the
house stood a row of tall Lombardy poplars:
a row of elms still leads up to the western entrance. The house is now about
one hundred and sixty years old, and with
proper care is good for another century. It was built in the old massive,

beamy fashion, wrought-iron nails being used throughout. A large barn was formerly connected with the premises, as well as a four-acre lot in the rear, now used as a playground by the students of Harvard University, and known as Holmes' Field. The successive owners of the estate have been: Barnabie Lamson, 1683; Nathaniel Sparhawk; a "Mr. ffox," 1707, probably the Rev. Jabez Fox of Woburn; Jonathan Hastings ("Yankee Jont."); Jonathan Hastings, Jr., for nearly thirty years steward of the college; Eliphalet Pearson, Professor of Oriental Literature; Judge Oliver Wendell; Rev. Abiel Holmes; and finally Harvard University, to which corporation the estate was sold in 1871 for fifty-five thousand dollars. Oliver Wendell had paid seven thousand dollars for it in 1807. Occupants of the house since the death of Abiel Holmes, have been Professor William Everett and Professor James Bradley Thayer.

Every New Englander knows, or ought to know, the following historical facts: That immediately after the battle of Lexington the neighboring population rallied to Cambridge by thousands; that what is now known as the Holmes House was selected by General-in-Chief Artemas Ward as his headquarters; that here was planned the occupation of Bunker Hill; that in the long, low dining-room, looking out through its heavily sashed windows on the Common, General Ward entertained Washington and his staff, the banquet being enlivened by patriotic songs; and finally that in this house the lamented General Warren rested on his way to Bunker Hill, and that here Benedict Arnold received his first commission. In "The Poet at the Breakfast-table" Dr. Holmes speaks of the tall mirror in which the British officers used to look at their red coats; and the deep, cunningly wrought arm-chair in which Lord Percy used to sit while his hair was dressing, and which he considerately protected with a cloth to save the silk covering embroidered by the poet's grandmother.

The study was, of course, a place of great attraction for young Oliver and his brother John. It was in that heavy-beamed room (the southeast ground-floor apartment), lined utterly, as to its walls, with books, that they

played and tumbled about among the leather-
coated folios and other o's, the like of which
in after years they would both learn to love
with the enthusiasm of the scholar and the
antiquary.　There is a tradition that the
many dints to be seen upon the floor of the
study were made by the butts of muskets
belonging to British soldiers; but of the
truth of this surmise no man for certain
knoweth.　The old house had its nooks and
crannies, and its mysteries.　In the "Autocrat" we learn of a certain odorous closet on
whose shelves used to lie bundles of sweet-
marjoram, and pennyroyal, and lavender, and
mint, and catnip, and where apples and
peaches were stored away to ripen.　Elsewhere we are told of wainscoats behind
which the mice were always scampering and
squeaking and rattling down the plaster; of
the cellar where the cold slug clung to the
walls, and the long white potato-shoots went
groping along the floor toward the light; and
finally of the garret with its flooring of lath
with ridges of mortar bulging out between
them ("which if you tread on you will go to
—the Lord have mercy on you! where *will*

you go to ?"), its old beams with the marks of the axe plainly visible, and its old decaying furniture — arm-chair, churn, spinning-wheel, andirons, cradle, and leather portmanteaus "like stranded porpoises, their mouths gaping in gaunt hunger for the food with which they used to be gorged to bulging repletion."

Just under the old garret are chambers, on the windows of which names had been scratched, some of them with romantic associations. The southeast chamber was used as a library-hospital, or museum, where disabled and veteran books were placed to end their days in dusty peace. Young Holmes seems to have spent some rainy days to good purpose in this book-infirmary. He says a work he found there on the "Negro Plot" in New York helped to implant a feeling of dislike of the negroes which it took Mr. Garrison a good many years to root out. Another book he found here was the novel "Thinks I To Myself," as well as an old work on alchemy, in which he sought in vain for information which would enable him to convert his lead-sinkers and the weights of the kitchen clock into good yellow gold.

In the *Atlantic Almanac* for 1868 Dr. Holmes writes in a charmingly colloquial and confidential style of the old garden and his experiences therein.   Such delightful egotism and *naïveté* disarm criticism and win our sympathy :—

"How long ago was it — Consule Jacobo Monrovio, — nay even more desperate than that, Consule Jacobo Madisonio — that I used to stray along the gravel walks of THE GAR-DEN ? It was a stately pleasure-place to me in those days. Since then my pupils have been stretched, like old India-rubber rings which have been used to hold one's female correspondence.   It turns out by adult meas-urement to be an oblong square of moderate dimensions, say a hundred by two hundred feet. There were old lilac bushes at the right of the entrance, and in the corner at the left that remarkable moral pear-tree which gave me one of my first lessons in life. Its fruit never ripened, but always rotted at the core just before it began to grow mellow. It was a vulgar, plebeian specimen at best, and was set there no doubt only to preach its annual sermon, a sort of ' Dudleian Lecture,' by a country preacher of small parts. But in the northern border was a high-bred Saint Michael pear-tree, which taught a lesson that all of gentle blood might take to heart; for its fruit used to get hard and dark, and break into unseemly cracks, so that when the lord of the harvest came for it it was like those rich men's sons we see too often, who have never ripened, but only rusted, hardened, and shrunken. We had peaches, lovely nectarines, and sweet white grapes, growing and coming to kindly maturity in those days; we should hardly expect them now, and yet there is no obvious change of climate. As for the garden-beds they were cared for by the Jonathan or Ephraim of the household, sometimes assisted by one Rule, a little old Scotch gardener, with a stippled face and a lively temper. Nothing but old-fashioned flowers in them, — hyacinths, pushing their green beaks through as soon as the snow was gone, or earlier; tulips, coming up in the shape of sugar 'cockles,' or cornucopiæ, — one was almost tempted to look to see whether nature had not packed one of those two-line 'sentiments' we remember so well in each of them;

peonies, butting their way bluntly through the loosened earth ; flower-de-luces (so I will call them, not otherwise) ; lilies, roses, damask, white, blush, cinnamon (these names served us then) ; larkspurs, lupines, and gorgeous hollyhocks. With these upper-class plants were blended, in republican fellowship, the useful vegetables of the working sort, — beets, handsome with dark red leaves ; carrots, with their elegant filigree foliage ; parsnips that clung to the earth like mandrakes ; radishes, illustrations of total depravity, a prey to every evil underground emissary of the powers of darkness ; onions, never easy until they are out of bed, so to speak, a communicative and companionable vegetable, with real genius for soups ; squash-vines with their generous fruits, the winter ones that will hang up ' agin the chimbly ' by-and-by, the summer ones, vase-like, as Hawthorne described them, with skins so white and delicate, when they are yet new-born, that one thinks of little sucking-pigs turned vegetables, like Daphne into a laurel, and then of tender human infancy, which Charles Lamb's favorite so calls to mind ; these, with melons, promis-

ing as 'first scholars,' but apt to put off ripen-
ing until the frost came and blasted their
vines and leaves, as if it had been a shower
of boiling water, were among the customary
growths of the garden.

"But Consuls Madisonius and Munrovius
left the seat of office, and Consuls Johannes
and Quincius, and Andreas, and Martinus,
and the rest, followed in their turn, until the
good Abraham sat in the curule chair. In
the meantime changes had been going on
under our old gambrel-roof, and The Garden
had been suffered to relapse slowly into a
state of wild nature. The haughty flower-
de-luces, the curled hyacinths, the perfumed
roses, had yielded their place to suckers from
locust-trees, to milkweed, burdock, plantain,
sorrel, purslain; the gravel walks, which
were to Nature as rents in her green garments, had been gradually darned over with
the million-threaded needles of her grasses,
until nothing was left to show that a garden
had been there.

"But the garden still existed in my memory; the walks were all mapped out there,
and the place of every herb and flower was
laid down as if on a chart.

"By that pattern I reconstructed The Garden, lost for a whole generation as much as Pompeii was lost; and in the consulate of our good Abraham, it was once more as it had been in the days of my childhood. It was not much to look upon for a stranger; but when the flowers came up in their old places the effect on me was something like what the widow of Nain may have felt when her dead son rose on the bier and smiled upon her.

"Nature behaved admirably, and sent me back all the little tokens of her affection she had kept so long. The same delegates from the underground fauna ate up my early radishes; I think I should have been disappointed if they had not. The same buff-colored bugs devoured my roses that I remembered of old. The aphis and the caterpillar and the squash-bug were cordial as ever, just as if nothing had happened to produce a coolness or an entire forgetfulness between us. But the butterflies came back too, and the bees and the birds.

" The yellow-birds used to be very fond of some sunflowers that grew close to the pear-tree with a moral. I remember their flitting about, golden in the golden light, over the golden flowers, as if they were flakes of curdled sunshine. Let us plant sunflowers, I said, and see whether the yellow-birds will not come back to them. Sure enough, the sunflowers had no sooner spread their disks, and begun to ripen their seeds, than the yellow-birds were once more twittering and fluttering around them."

The references to the sandy sterility of the soil of the old garden remind one of a passage in "The Poet at the Breakfast Table," wherein Dr. Holmes facetiously says that he might, if he chose, find an excuse for his moral shortcomings and peccadillos in the characteristics of this region. He says that the pests of the soil induced in him Manichæan ways of thinking.

Never were there two boys who drank in enjoyment at every pore more incessantly than did young Oliver and John Holmes. The latter has as gay and effervescent a spirit as his more widely-known brother. The larks they engaged in as boys were undoubtedly numerous and racy. There are some hints of these in the writings of Dr. Oliver W. Holmes. The following lines from a college poem * of his, entitled "Scenes from an Unpublished Play," have about them an aroma and suggestion of "high old times" : —

"*Back-room at Porter's,* — Dick, *solus.*
" I'm not well to-night — methinks the fumes
  Of overheated punch have something dimmed
  The cerebellum or pineal gland,
  Or where the soul sits regent."

There are a good many glimpses, too, of first school-days in the poet's writings. His first school-teacher was Ma'am Hancock, whose cottage (called the "ten-footer") stood close by the district school-house. Another school-mistress of his was Dame Prentiss, in whose low-studded room stood, we are told, a pail full of drinking water, flavored with the white pine of which the pail was made, and a brown mug "out of which one Edmund, a red-faced and curly-haired boy, was averred to have bitten a fragment in his haste to drink." The old lady had a long willow stick with which she could reach refractory pupils. We

* Published in the *Collegian*, and not reprinted.

further learn that there were certain infantine love-makings going on beneath the good dame's nose, but of which she was, of course, entirely oblivious.

Holmes says that as a child he was afraid of the tall masts of ships and schooners, and used to hide his eyes from them. Another source of terror to him was a great wooden hand, the sign of a glove-maker who lived a mile or two from Cambridge. One of the luxuries of the boy was to lie in bed in the early morning and listen to the creaking of the heavily-loaded wood-sleds drawn slowly over the shrieking snow by the large, patient oxen. It was the custom in those days for the Sabbath to begin with Saturday night, and on such occasions playthings must be put away and work cease, while a solemn hush and awe fell upon the household — a silence only broken by the continuous chirping of the evening crickets mingled with the batrachian hymns from the neighboring swamp.

One of the great holidays for boys was the College Commencement, which will be described in the next chapter. Moreover, about the time of the college vacation in May came two Boston holidays, styled "Nigger 'lection" and "Artillery Election,"—the former so called because on that day (the last Wednesday in May) the colored people were allowed to engage in the festivities on the Common, the occasion being the assembling of the Legislature. Both days somewhat resembled country fairs. The Tremont Street mall was then (as it still is to-day) appropriated by penny refreshment venders and small wonder-workers. It was lilac time, and everybody carried huge bunches of the delicious blossoms, "with heart-shaped leaves of rich green," and overmastering odor. The Cambridge boys had grand fun on these occasions. "A bunch of 'laylocks' and a 'lection bun used to make us happy in old times," wrote Dr. Holmes once, as he called up the happy days of his boyhood. And there was something stronger than water drank on the occasion; the rummy perfume of egg-pop and "black joke," mingled with whiffs of peppermint and checkerberry from the candy stalls, and the floating fragrance of the omnipresent lilacs.

Of the books read by the boys in Abiel Holmes' household his son Oliver has enumerated Miss Edgeworth's "Frank," and "Parents' Assistant," "Original Poems," "Evenings at Home," and "Cheap Repository Tracts." A book whose moral made a great impression on his mind was a pleasant story called "Eyes and No Eyes," which tells of a certain discontented boy who thought that he could have improved on the arrangement of the seasons, but finally discovered that he had an equal love for each of them.

But to return to school experiences. In the brief description which the poet has given of Dame Prentiss' school, he mentions the existence of "a great forfeit-basket filled with its miscellaneous waifs and *deodands.*" This last word is one of the few in Dr. Holmes' writings which seem to show traces of his legal studies. In legal language a deodand was a personal chattel (a cart or a horse, *e.g.*) which had occasioned the death of a rational creature, and been forfeited to the crown. The deodands, or forfeits, of Dame Prentiss' school were probably instruments designed for the capture and imprisonment, or torture,

of those wonderful little creatures which so
attract the school-boy's itching palm, and so
allure his fancy, — *i. e.* flies !   After leaving
this school young Holmes became a pupil of
Master William Biglow, mentioned by Duyckinck as a writer of considerable merit.

From a paper by Dr. Holmes in the Proceedings of the Massachusetts Historical
Society for September, 1865, and from an
article by him entitled "Cinders from the
Ashes," published in the *Atlantic Monthly*
for January, 1869, the following facts concerning his experiences at the Cambridgeport school have been culled : —

This school was established in 1819 by the
efforts of Dr. James P. Chaplin and others.
It was about a mile from the Holmes mansion to the school, and the way led through
that thinly-inhabited, woody, marshy, huckle-
berryish tract which many citizens of Cambridge, not yet very old, are fond of telling
you about, — doubtless because it was the
scene of so many of their childish adventures
and sports.   There were very few houses
then between Old Cambridge and "The
Port."   The school was limited to thirty

students, was sometimes called the Academy, and was considered to offer much better advantages than other schools of the time. It stood, during most of the period when it was attended by young Holmes, on the left hand side of Prospect Street as you turn down from Main Street. Holmes was ten years old when he began to attend the school, and he remained there for about five years, leaving it in 1824, to go to the Andover Phillips Academy. The first instructor at the Port School was Edward S. Dickinson, a graduate of Harvard College, and at that time a student of medicine. Other instructors when Holmes attended were the Rev. Samuel Barrett, the Rev. Ezra Stiles Gannett, Mr. John Frost, Mr. Edward Frost, the Rev. Nathaniel Gage, and Mr. Thaddeus Bowman Bigelow. The boys of the school were a good deal given to fighting. Their champion, a nephew of Washington Allston, had at least two combats with outside boys, who were styled Port-chucks in the parlance of the Academy boys. One of the poet's schoolmates at the "Port" was Richard Henry Dana, Jr., and another was — the poet himself shall tell who. (See his magazine article, "Cinders from the Ashes.")

"Sitting on the girls' benches, conspicuous among the school-girls of unlettered origin by that look which rarely fails to betray hereditary and congenital culture, was a young person of very nearly my own age. She came with the reputation of being 'smart,' as we should have called it, 'clever' as we say nowadays. This was Margaret Fuller, the only one among us who, like Jean Paul, like the Duke, like Bettina, has slipped the cable of the more distinctive name to which she was anchored, and floats on the waves of speech as Margaret. Her air to her schoolmates was marked by a certain stateliness and distance, as if she had other thoughts than theirs and was not of them. She was a great student and a great reader of what she used to call 'náw-véls.' I remember her so well as she appeared at school and later, that I regret that she had not been faithfully given to canvas or marble in the day of her best looks. None know her aspect who have not seen her living. Margaret, as I remember her at school and afterwards, was tall, fair-complexioned, with a watery, aquamarine lustre in her light eyes, which she used to make small, as one does who looks at the sunshine. A remarkable point about her was that long flexile neck, arching and undulating in strange sinuous movements, which one who loved her would compare to those of a swan, and one who loved her not to those of the ophidian who tempted our common mother. Her talk was affluent, magisterial, *de haut en bas*, some would say euphuistic, but surpassing the talk of women in breadth and audacity. Her face kindled, and reddened, and dilated in every feature as she spoke, and, as I once saw her in a fine storm of indignation at the supposed ill-treatment of a relative, showed itself capable of something resembling what Milton calls the viraginian aspect."

A school essay of Margaret's was brought to the poet's father for examination. When young Oliver took it up he found that it began thus: "It is a *trite* remark." Alas! he did not know the meaning of this word. It was, he says, a crushing discovery of her superiority.

After five years' study at the Cambridgeport school, Holmes was taken to Andover
to study a year in Phillips Academy as a
preparation for college. At this time he was
an energetic and vivacious youngster, full of
all sorts of fun and mischief, with "tendencies in the way of flageolets and flutes,"
and a weakness for pistols and guns and
cigars, which latter he would hide in the
barrel of his pistol, where maternal eyes
would never dare to look for them.

In due time parents and "slightly nostal-
gic boy" jogged away in the old carriage for
Andover, up the old West Cambridge road,
now North Avenue, past the powder-house,
and on through country lanes and roads till
their destination was reached. They stopped,
just at the entrance of the central village, at
a low two-story white house, the residence
of one of the theological professors. The
carriage and his fond parents left him at
last, and he watched the retreating vehicle
rising and sinking along the road until at
length it entirely disappeared. He was the
most homesick boy that ever lived. His case
excited sympathy. " There was an ancient,

faded old lady in the house," he says, " very kindly but very deaf, rustling about in dark autumnal foliage of silk or other murmurous fabric, somewhat given to snuff, but a very worthy gentlewoman of the poor-relation variety. She comforted me, I well remember, but not with apples, and stayed me, but not with flagons. She went in her benevolence, and taking a blue and white soda-powder, mingled the same in water, and encouraged me to drink the result. It might be a specific for sea-sickness, but it was not for home-sickness. The *fizz* was a mockery, and the saline refrigerant struck a colder chill to my heart. I did not disgrace myself, however, and a few days cured me, as a week on the water often cures sea-sickness."

One of the masters who sat in the dreary old academy building was the Rev. Samuel Horatio Stearns, an excellent and kindly man who won the little Cambridge boy's heart. On the side of the long school-room was a large clock-dial, bearing these words : —

YOUTH IS THE SEED-TIME OF LIFE.

Mr. Holmes gives us some account of his

schoolmates at Andover. One of them "with a fuliginous complexion, a dilating and whitening nostril, and a singularly malignant scowl," years afterwards committed some act of murderous violence, and ended his days in a madhouse. The delight of this ferocious youngster was to kick our Oliver's shins under the bench. Another little fellow, upon whom young Holmes' eye was riveted from the moment of his entrance, had black hair and very black eyes, and his gaze was fastened to his book as if he had been reading a will that made him heir to a million. This was the future distinguished Greek scholar and Bible commentator, Prof. Horatio Balch Hackett. Another classmate was the well-known Phineas Barnes, of Portland, Maine.

Among the professors were Dr. Porter, Dr. Woods, and the well-known Prof. Moses Stuart, — the latter tall, lean, Roman-faced, impressive, the very incarnation of a noble Roman orator, carrying his broadcloth cloak over his arm like a toga, and looking more like a walking statue than a man.

The boys had their sports, visits to Indian Ridge, climbing the hills, swimming in the dark and rapid Shawsheen or in the not very distant Merrimack, etc. One of young Holmes' exercises was a very creditable translation from Virgil. It is preserved in his complete poetical works.

Then there was a visit with a classmate to Haverhill, where our Cambridge lad saw the door of the ancient parsonage with the bullet-hole in it, through which Benjamin Rolfe, the minister, was shot by the Indians on the 29th of August, 1703.

An absorbing occupation of the boys was watching one of the tutors who had had a dream that he would fall dead while he was praying. He regarded it as a warning, and asked the boys to come to see him in turn before he died. "More than one boy kept his eye on him during his public devotions, possessed by the same feeling the man had that followed Van Amburgh about with the expectation, let us not say hope, of seeing the lion bite his head off sooner or later."

Years afterward, in 1867, Dr. Holmes revisited the scene of his year's schooling, and gives us, in the same article from which we have quoted, a pleasant account of his ex-

periences.   He says the ghost of a boy was
at his side as he wandered among the places
he knew so well : "'Two tickets to Boston,'
I said to the man at the station.

"But the little ghost whispered, ' *When
you leave this place you leave me behind you.*'

"'*One* ticket to Boston, if you please.
Good-by, little ghost.'"

CHAPTER III.

HARVARD.

In this country of monotonous uniformity of social classes there is a tendency to make the most of such exclusive associations as are not obnoxious to the spirit of democracy. Probably in no other country in the world do college men cling to each other through life with such tenacity as they do here; and college men know that there is no other social relation in life so purely enjoyable and valuable to them as is the gentle free-masonry of the college class, both in undergraduate and postgraduate life. The Harvard College class of 1829 has been fortunate in possessing a poet (Dr. Holmes) who is an enthusiastic college man, and has made his class unique by his poems in its honor. "The Boys of '29" he delights to call them; and he is the greatest boy of them all. His whole life is pervaded by college associations. How delightful to perpetuate through a lifetime those first fresh and indefinable feelings of our college life, — days of divine leisure when we drank deep, unquenchable draughts from the fountains of the wisdom of the ages, and heard afar off the indistinguishable roar of life, content, as we thought, to eat of that sweet lotus fruit of knowledge forever!

In 1825, immediately after his return home from Phillips Academy, young Holmes entered Harvard, the class containing the then unusually large number of seventy-one freshmen, fifty-eight of whom graduated. Among the professors whose names appear on the pages of the four little college catalogues issued from 1826 to 1829, inclusive, there is the name of only one man now living, and that is Dr. Oliver Stearns, of the class of 1826. In his class poem of 1879, "Vestigia Quinque Retrorsum," Dr. Holmes has given a pleasing sketch of President Kirkland and the college professors of his day : —

"Look back, O comrades, with your faded eyes,
And see the phantoms as I bid them rise.
Whose smile is that?   Its pattern Nature gave,
A sunbeam dancing in a dimpled wave ;

Kirkland alone such grace from Heaven could
    win,
His features radiant as the soul within;
That smile would let him through Saint Peter's
    gate
While sad-eyed martyrs had to stand and wait.
Here flits mercurial *Farrar;* standing there,
See mild, benignant, cautious, learned *Ware,*
And sturdy, patient, faithful, honest *Hedge,*
Whose grinding logic gave our wits their edge;
Ticknor, with honeyed voice and courtly grace;
And *Willard* larynxed like a double bass;
And *Channing* with his bland superior look,
Cool as a moonbeam on a frozen brook,
While the pale student, shivering in his shoes,
Sees from his theme the turgid rhetoric ooze;
And the born soldier, fate decreed to wreak
His martial manhood on a class in Greek,
Popkin ! How that explosive name recalls
The grand old Busby of our ancient halls !
Such faces looked from Skippon's grim platoons,
Such figures rode with Ireton's stout dragoons;
He gave his strength to learning's gentle charms,
But every accent sounded ' Shoulder arms !' "

At the time Holmes entered college the
spirit of the age was already setting against
ministers and "orthodoxy." In 1826 Am-

herst College was founded for the express purpose of counteracting the liberal tendencies of Harvard, and Henry Ware was severely denounced for not preaching eternal punishment to the students. It is well to remember these facts when we would seek the causes of the life-long warfare against the bigotries of "orthodoxy" which has been waged by Dr. Holmes.

At college he delivered the poem before the Hasty Pudding Club, had the poem at Exhibition, also one at Commencement, and was chosen as the class poet. Among the classmates of Holmes were Professor Benjamin Peirce, the eminent mathematician and astronomer (who, by the way, was born in the same year with Holmes, *i. e.*, 1809); Judge Benjamin R. Curtis of the United States Supreme Court; Rev. Dr. James Freeman Clarke, author and clergyman (the "good Saint James"); Judge George T. Bigelow of the Massachusetts Supreme Court; the Hon. George T. Davies; the Rev. Dr. Chandler Robbins; the Rev. William H. Channing; and the Rev. Samuel Francis Smith, author of "My Country, 'tis of

Thee," and the hymn, "The Morning Light is Breaking." Dr. Holmes has thus wittily spoken of his classmate, Smith : —

" And there's a nice youngster of excellent pith, —
Fate tried to conceal him by naming him Smith ;
But he shouted a song for the brave and the
    free, —
Just read on his medal, ' My country,' ' of
    thee !' "

Charles Sumner was a member of the class of 1830, and the historian Motley belonged to the class of 1831. Motley roomed at the historical Brattle House, amid elegant surroundings. Dr. Holmes has said of him that he was probably the youngest student in college. An unusual affection and intimacy between Holmes and Motley continued through life, and the former has written the life of his historian friend. In a communication addressed to the Massachusetts Historical Society, Dr. Holmes said : —

" Motley was more nearly the ideal of a young poet than any boy — for he was only a boy as yet — who sat on the benches of the college chapel. His finely shaped and expressive features, his large, luminous eyes, his dark waving hair, the singularly spirited set of his head, which was most worthy of note for its shapely form and poise, his well-outlined figure, gave promise of his manly beauty, and commended him even to those who could not fully appreciate the richer endowments of which they were only the outward signature."

Of another of his college-mates, Charles Chauncy Emerson, Dr. Holmes has thus spoken: "A beautiful, high-souled, pure, exquisitely delicate nature in a slight but finely wrought mortal frame, he was for me the very ideal of an embodied celestial intelligence. I may venture to mention a trivial circumstance because it points to the character of his favorite reading, which was likely to be guided by the same tastes as his brother's, and may have been specially directed by him. Coming into my room one day, he took up a copy of Hazlitt's British Poets. He opened it at the poem of Andrew Marvell's, entitled "The Nymph Complaining for the Death of her Fawn," which he read to me with delight irradiating his expressive features. The lines remained with me, or many of them, from that hour : —

> 'Had it lived long, it would have been
> Lilies without, roses within.'

I felt as many have felt after being with his brother, Ralph Waldo, that I had entertained an angel visitant. The Fawn of Marvell's imagination survives in my memory as the fitting image to recall this beautiful youth; a soul glowing like the rose of morning with enthusiasm, a character white as the lilies in its purity."

It is, of course, impossible now to produce a complete picture of the undergraduate life of Harvard College as it was when Holmes was a student. But that excellent journal, *The Harvard Register*, (meteoric in its brilliancy), brought to light many invaluable reminiscences of life at Harvard fifty years ago, and we shall thankfully avail ourselves of them here. And first a word about college societies. One of these, to which Motley and John Osborne Sargent belonged, was called "The Knights of the Square Table." In 1829 Holmes was Curator "Medicati

Apparatus," in the waggish club called the "Med. Facs." There were some twenty burlesque professors; Cornelius C. Felton being Bugologiae et Cornucopialogiae Professor; Ezra Stiles Gannett, Craniologiae Professor, etc.

The first meeting of the year was held in an upper room in Hollis, which, as we are informed by Mr. Henry Winthrop Sargent, was draped in black cotton, and decorated with death's-heads and cross-bones in chalk: a table also hung with black extended lengthwise through the room. In the centre on a raised seat sat the Praeses, and on either side of him various Professores and Professores Adjuncti, clad in black, and wearing the flat Oxford cap. Near at hand stood two gensd'armes, usually the two strongest men in the class, entirely clothed in flesh-colored tights, the oldest holding the celebrated club, "Intonitans Bolus," and the younger the smaller Bolus. Upon the stairs were crowds of Juniors, from whom some twenty or thirty were to be initiated into the society. The initiation consisted either in answering disagreeable questions put by the Professores, or in doing such things as standing on your head, crawling about the floor with the collar-bone of an ass over your neck, singing Mother Goose melodies, or making an oration in one of the dead languages.

Holmes belonged while in college to another small temporary association called the Διαφημίζονοι, or Notables. (See the Life of Benjamin R. Curtis, by George T. Curtis.) Another member of this little debating society was William Henry Channing.

According to the Rev. Cazneau Palfrey, the Hasty Pudding Club then met at the rooms of its members. Chairs were obtained from neighboring rooms, and the pudding was prepared by a worthy matron of the village, who was familiarly spoken of in the club as Sister Stimson, and was regarded as a *quasi* member of the society.

The "providers" of the evening slung their two huge pots of boiling mush, or porridge, upon a stout pole, and resting the ends thereof upon their shoulders mounted gallantly to the room where the members were assembled, — often in the third or fourth story. Strange to say there is no tradition of anybody having been scalded to death while engaged in this perilous feat. A bowl of pudding was always carried as a propitiatory offering to the officer of the entry in which the meeting was held, and after adjournment the occupants of neighboring rooms were invited to partake of the generous abundance of pudding that still remained.*

Of course there were the usual practical jokes and students' pranks. Hazing in a mild form was in vogue, and that there were nocturnal *deciperes* goes without saying. General H. K. Oliver, in his hilarious and inimitable style, tells of "the raiding-for, the slaying, the unfeathering (we did not pause to eviscerate), the roasting, — tied to a string, and twirled before an open fire, at No. 19 Hollis Hall, — and the festal surfeit over the well-cooked *corpus mortuum* of a proud bird known to naturalists as the *Meleagris Gallopavo*, — *Anglicè*, Gobbler! All the need-

* For further particulars of the Club see "The Harvard Book," and an article by the author on "Undergraduate Life in Harvard," published in *The Continent* for January 10, 1883.

fuls for the due spread of the table, and all fitting condiments were ensconced in a trap-door-covered box beneath the floor, the artillery of prying eyes of proctors wise being foiled by a barricade of blankets so effectual that total darkness seemed to reign within."

It was justly considered a great affliction to be obliged to attend prayers before daylight in winter in a bitterly cold room, and many tricks were played by the students to testify their repugnance.

On one occasion the candles were slyly cut and pieces of lead inserted and covered over with tallow: of course the lights went out when the lead was reached. On another occasion "pull-crackers" were fastened to the lids of the Bible, and when the book was opened they exploded with loud reports. One day a hog's head appeared on the Bible, to the astonishment and horror of the officiating clergyman.

In further illustration of the college life of those days, Dr. A. P. Peabody tells us of the Spartan simplicity of the college rooms, ten dollars being a fair auction price for the furniture of the carpetless studies. The fires were of wood, and were lighted by flint, steel, and tinder-box. "Almost every room had, too, among its *transmittenda* a cannon-ball, supposed to have been derived from the arsenal, which on very cold days was heated to a red heat, and placed as a calorific radiant on some extemporized metallic stand; while at other seasons it was often utilized by being rolled down-stairs at such time as might most nearly bisect a proctor's night-sleep." The only conveyance to Boston was a two-horse stage-coach, which ran twice each day.

A great institution in those days was the Harvard Washington Corps, or college military company, for which the State lent arms and equipments. There were so few college sports then — no base-ball, no cricket, no boating, no gymnasium — that the corps attracted great attention. The brigade band contained twenty-eight pieces. The uniform consisted of the prescribed college dress, which was dark Oxford mixed-gray single-breasted coats, with three crow's feet on the sleeve to distinguish a Senior, two for a Junior, one for a Sophomore, and none for a Freshman; the skirts of the coat were cut away like those of our present dress-coats, White cross-belts were worn ; and the officers had felt caps with black leather visors and black fountain plumes : they also wore gilt buttons, gold epaulets, white trousers, white sword-belt, and scarlet silk sash. The motto of the corps was, " Tam Marti quam Mercurio."

One of the dormitories of the days we are speaking of was an old three-story wooden building called the Devil's Den, which stood just south of the spot where is now the Unitarian Church. Flutes and other worldly musical instruments were generally reprobated by orthodox clergymen, and General Henry Kemble Oliver tells us that he used to conceal his flute beneath his feather-bed, his father having forbidden him to play upon the heathen instrument. The Pierian Sodality was in existence, and there was excellent singing by the college choir. Prayers twice a day, — in winter by candle-light in a cold room ; two services on Sunday ; commons eaten in University Hall, which then had a broad piazza in front, with wide steps at each end. The curriculum and *ars docendi* were similar to the same in an old-fashioned Western college at the present day, and the feeling between students and professors was one of antagonism.

A good recitation story is told by General Oliver of Professor Popkin (" old Pop "). He was accustomed to call up the lads in alphabetical order. "But somebody had amazed· him by hinting that the innocents with whom he had to deal might possibly be in the habit of counting noses, and preparing accordingly, as was the lamentable fact. He had, on a certain day, closed recitation with the W's, and it was expected that he would next begin with the A's; and therefore some twenty A's, B's, and C's, — but very few else, — got 'booked,' the fellows at the tail taking it easy. In due time we gathered together: the good man came in, and taking his seat, earnestly gazed awhile (his right foot over his left knee, and his right shin rejoicing under its customary manipulation) at Todd Adams. ·Then whisking round with a sudden jerk, he shrieked out, with a grim and mischievous chuckle, 'Williams, now I've got you!' and so he had. A roar of laughter rent

the room ; and Williams, with sundry other
bankrupts at the tail end of the division, took
the 'deadest of screws.'"

In the year 1827, while in college, Holmes
became joint author with John Osborne Sargent and Park Benjamin of a little volume,
entitled "Poetical Illustrations of the Athenæum Gallery of Paintings." The poems are
chiefly satirical in cast. In the copy owned
by the Athenæum Library in Boston, the
poem called "The Boy with the Golden
Locks" is marked in pencil with the name
O. W. Holmes ; the boy of the painting was
Samuel Eliot, and the artist R. Peale. It is
stated in the "Memorial History of Boston"
that the first attempt at an art gallery in
Boston was made in 1826, when a collection
of casts from the antique, the gift of Augustus
Thorndike, together with one or two portraits
of benefactors of the Athenæum, were exhib-
ited by that institution. The next year
(1827) the first regular exhibition of paintings
and sculpture was opened to the public. It
curiously marks the advance made in enlightened views of women when we are told by
Miss Sarah Freeman Clarke, that at the time

this exhibition was opened " a joyous whisper
went round that ladies might go to it unat-
tended by gentlemen ! "

The great event of college life was Commencement (Class Day as yet was not, that
institution coming in with President Quincy).
The festival of Commencement resembled a
modern fair. Listen to this description of
Dr. Holmes : —

" The fair plain (the Common), not then, as
now, cut up into cattle-pens by the ugliest of
known fences, swarmed with the joyous crowds.
The ginger-beer carts rang their bells and
popped their bottles, the fiddlers played
Money Musk over and over and over, the
sailors danced the double-shuffle, the gentlemen of the city capered in lusty jigs, the town
ladies even took a part in the graceful exercise, the confectioners rattled red and white
sugar-plums, long sticks of candy, sugar and
burnt almonds into their brass scales, the
wedges of pie were driven into splitting
mouths, the mountains of (clove-besprinkled)
hams were cut down as Fort Hill is being
sliced to-day ; the hungry feeders sat still and
concentrated about the boards where the

grosser viands were served, while the milk flowed from cracking cocoanuts, the fragrant muskmelons were cloven into new-moon crescents, and the great watermelons showed their cool pulps sparkling and roseate as the dewy fingers of Aurora."

From a paper styled a " Sketch in Sentimental Antiquarianism " (in " The Harvard Book "), written by our genial friend John Holmes, the brother of the poet, we obtain many pleasant glimpses of the informal and subordinate features of Commencement as it appeared fifty or sixty years ago. A day or two before the eventful occasion, spaces for tents were measured on the Common by the town agent, and the number of each marked in the sod. Everything was in a delightful tumult. Old friends and relatives returned. " On Tuesday, after the nearer relatives had arrived, there might drop in at evening a third cousin of a wife's half-brother from Agawam, or an uncle of a brother-in-law's step-sister from Contoocoŏk, to reknit the family ties. The runaway apprentice, who was ready to condone offences and accept hospitality, was referred to the barn, as well as the Indian from Mr. Wheelock's Seminary, whose equipment was an Indian catechism and a bow and arrow, with which latter he expected to turn a fugitive penny by shooting at a mark on the morrow." . . . At night, "if any villager awoke from troublous dreams of pillage, the sounds from the Common as of 'armorers with busy hammers closing rivets up,' in other words, the blows of shadowy tent-builders, refreshed his moral nature, and anon he sank pleasantly into festive visions. . . . At Miss Chadbourne's, the numerous lodgers in the garret pensively studied by the light of the lantern which served as police the antiquities suspended from the rafters, or stowed under the eaves. The disabled spinning wheel, the old bonnet that had attended Governor Belcher's first Commencement, the screen with the figures of Shadrach, Meshach, and Abednego, that had been placed too near the fire, — these and other articles had been perused to the verge of desperation, when a sudden blank — and lo! the great day had come."

The tents were upon the western side of the college yard, and, "having opposite them various stands and shows, made a street which, by nightfall, was paved with water-melon rinds, peach-stones, and various débris, on a ground of straw, — all flavored with rum and tobacco-smoke. The atmosphere thus created in the interests of literature was to the true devotee of Commencement what the flavor of the holocaust was to the pious ancient." In the afternoon all was freedom and gayety. "The rough village doctor, though witnessing the abominable breach of hygienic law everywhere, felt the cheering influence of the day, and his old mare with perplexity missed half her usual allowance of cowhide. The dry, sceptical village lawyer returned from dinner at Miss Chadbourne's to his dusty office in his best mood, prepared to deny everything advanced by anybody, and demand proof. On the Common the Natick Indians, having made large gain by their bows and arrows, proceeded to a retired spot, and silently and successively achieved the process of inebriation." Such were some of the features of Commencement at Harvard sixty years ago, and such were probably the features of that particular Commencement Day of which the Autocrat has written the following :—

"' 'Tis the first year of stern 'Old Hickory's' rule,
When our good Mother lets us out of school,
Half glad, half sorrowing, it must be confessed,
To leave her quiet lap, her bounteous breast,
Armed with our dainty, ribbon-tied degrees,
Pleased and yet pensive, exiles and A. B.'s."

For a year after leaving college Holmes studied law at Harvard under Judge Story and Mr. Ashmun (1830). At the end of that time he decided to abandon the study of Blackstone and Chitty for medicine, the profession of his grandfather, David Holmes of Woodstock. He has remarked that he can hardly say what induced him to give up law for medicine, but that he had from the first regarded his legal studies as an experiment. He has also said, half jocosely, that but for the seductive attractions of college journalism, he might have applied himself with more diligence to his legal studies, and carried a green bag in place of a stethoscope and a thermometer to this day.

It is said that it was at one time the hope of his father that he might study for the ministry, and it is thought that one of the reasons why he was sent to school at Andover was that he might acquire a liking for theology in the pious atmosphere of that place.

Oliver Wendell Holmes in the pulpit! The very idea raises a merry laugh, and we seem to see a congregation of upturned faces, each irradiated by the broadest of grins. And yet there is a good deal of the preacher in Holmes: his essays are lay sermons.

His first taste of types and proof-sheets ("attack of author's lead-poisoning," he calls it) he got while studying law. To the six months' college periodical, called the *Collegian*, he contributed twenty-five poems, some of which are retained in his complete editions, and have not been surpassed by his later productions. Certainly he has written no humorous poems more irresistibly droll than "The Dorchester Giant," "Evening by a Tailor," "The Spectre Pig," and "The Height of the Ridiculous." That the editors and readers of the *Collegian* appreciated the unique merit of the verses is evident from the fact that in the index to the periodical all of Holmes' pieces are indicated by an asterisk. Perhaps they did not know that for clear and unstudied humor, a sense of which creeps slowly and delightfully throughout the whole frame, the poems of their young contributor were superior to those of Hood, the great humorist of that day. But we know this now. The chief editor of the *Collegian* was the genial John Osborne Sargent, who wrote bright and vivacious prose and poetical pieces under the *nom de plume* of " Charles Sperry." William H. Simmons was " Lockfast," and Theodore W. Snow figured as "Geoffrey la Touche." Assistant editors or regular contributors were Epes Sargent (brother of J. O. Sargent), Robert Habersham, Jr., of Boston, and Frederick W. Brune, of Baltimore.

The first poem of Holmes in the collection, probably the first ever published by him (" Runaway Ballads," February, 1830), is a serio-comic piece in two parts, with just a spice of naughtiness in it, to be generously overlooked in a young man : —

I.

" Wake from thy slumbers, Isabel, the stars are in
    the sky,
And night has hung her silver lamp, to light our
    altar by;

The flowers have closed their fading leaves, and
   droop upon the plain,
O wake thee, and their dying hues shall blush to
   life again."

II.

"Get up! get up! Miss Polly Jones, the tandem's
   at the door;
Get up, and shake your lovely bones, it's twelve
   o'clock and more;
The chaises they have rattled by, and nothing
   stirs around,
And all the world but you and me are snoring
   safe and sound.

I've got my uncle's bay, and trotting Peggy, too,
I've lined their tripes with oats and hay, and now
     for love and you;
The lash is curling in the air, and I am at your
   side,
To-morrow you are Mrs. Snaggs, my bold and
   blooming bride."

Another poem (like the foregoing, nèver
republished) bears the title " Romance ": —

"O! she was a maid of a laughing eye,
   And she lived in a garret cold and high;
   And he was a threadbare whiskered beau,
   And he lived in a cellar damp and low."

The *Collegian* had been preceded in the year 1827 by *The Harvard Register* (the first of that name), which, although it had no genius like Holmes on its staff, was yet supported in a brilliant manner by a corps of contributors, many of whom afterwards became famous. Among these were C. C. Felton, Robert C. Winthrop, C. C. Emerson, Robert Rantoul, George S. Hillard, and James Freeman Clarke, — all undergraduates in the college. It is pleasant to see the Rev. James Freeman Clarke in the rôle of a humorous writer, — namely, in a piece entitled "The Miseries of the Spectacle Family ; or, the Near-sighted." The lurking humor which has always characterized him had, very appropriately, a livelier and more piquant spirit in that bright heyday of youth.

It was about 1829 or 1830 that Holmes wrote his stirring lyric, "Old Ironsides," — this term being the popular nickname for the battle-ship *Constitution.* The old war vessel appeared in Boston harbor on the Fourth of July, 1828, firing a salute in honor of the day, and also firing the popular heart with new enthusiasm for herself. In turning over the files of the *Boston Advertiser*, the writer found the following sentence in an editorial of July 8, 1828. It neatly sums up the popular sentiment concerning the old ship: "We may safely challenge the annals of the world to name the ship that has done so much to fill the measure of her country's glory." It was found that some of the timbers were so unsound that it was proposed by the government to break her up. Holmes voiced the protest of the whole land in his poem; the verses ran through every newspaper in the Union, and were circulated on handbills in Washington, so that Mr. Secretary Branch, unwilling to incur the odium of carrying out his previous intentions, gave orders to have the ship overhauled and repaired, which was accordingly done. The curious will find much entertaining information about the *Constitution* in Drake's "Old Landmarks of Boston." Dr. Holmes tells us elsewhere that he wrote the poem, "Old Ironsides," by a window in the white chamber of the Gambrel-roofed House, "*stans pede in uno*, pretty nearly." But however hastily written, it is certainly one of the finest patriotic lyrics in the language, and thrills the heart as only works of the highest genius can do. Standing, as it does, at the portal of Dr. Holmes' complete poetical works, it forms a most spirited introduction to these. The genius of Holmes, like that of Emerson, seems to have flowered out at once into vigorous poetical expression without the necessity of a long apprenticeship to the art.

CHAPTER IV.

PHYSICIAN AND PROFESSOR.

FROM the autumn of 1830 to the spring of
1833 Holmes studied medicine in Boston,
his instructors being Drs. Channing, Ware,
Lewis, Otis, Jackson, and others.   For Dr.
James Jackson he always had a deep attachment, and has repeatedly written about him
in terms of affection and reverence.*   By his
marriage, Dr. Holmes afterwards became the
son-in-law of Dr. Jackson's brother.   The
life of a young saw-bones is hardly compat-
ible with the cultivation of poetry.   There
is unfortunately, but undeniably, something

* He says of him that, "while he studied his patients
with all the inquisitiveness which belongs to science,
he cared for every individual among them as one who
thought only of them and their welfare.   Those who
enjoyed the privilege of his teaching would bear testimony that no man more entirely forgot himself in his
duties; that he taught them to rely on no oracular
authority, but to look the facts before them in the face;
that he educated them for knowledge beyond his own;
and that, while they recognized in him a master of his

hardening and materializing (almost animal-
izing) in the first acquaintance of a medical
student with dissections, and in the investi-
gation of the repulsive diseases of the human
body.* In the few literary productions of
Holmes published from 1830–33 we seem to
find traces of this influence.

In the *New England Magazine* appeared
about this time the poem, "My Aunt," as
well as some boyish prose pieces, one de-
scribing a little street flirtation, and another
being a bit of antiquarian talk on books, — a
topic on which Dr. Holmes always likes fondly
to expatiate.   He is a genuine bibliophile, and
when in Europe as a student eagerly indulged
the inherited passion.   "What a delight"
(he says in a little-known pamphlet) "in
the pursuit of the rarities which the eager
book-hunter follows with the scent of a

art, they left him with minds fully open to new convic-
tions from fresh sources of truth."

* Dr. Holmes has said that he began the study of
medicine as most young men do, — with a quickened
pulse at sight of the grinning skeletons of the school,
and with his cheeks reflecting the whiteness of the hospital sheets, — but that these sights soon became the
merest commonplace to him.

beagle! Shall I ever forget that rainy day in Lyons, that dingy bookshop, where I found the Aëtius, long missing from my Artis Medicæ Principes, and where I bought for a small pecuniary consideration, though it was marked *rare*, and was really *très rare*, the Aphorisms of Hippocrates, edited by and with a preface from the hand of Francis Rabelais? And the vellum-bound Tulpius, which I came upon in Venice, afterwards my only reading when imprisoned in quarantine at Marseilles, so that the two hundred and twenty-eight cases he has recorded are, many of them, to this day still fresh in my memory. And the Schenckius,—the folio filled with *casus rariores*, which had strayed in among the rubbish of the book-stall on the boulevard, —and the noble old Vesalius, with its grand frontispiece not unworthy of Titian, and the fine old Ambroise Paré, long waited for even in Paris and long ago, and the colossal Spigelius with his eviscerated beauties, and Dutch Bidloo with its miracles of fine engraving and bad dissection, and Italian Mascagni, the despair of all would-be imitators, and pre-Adamite John de Ketam, and antediluvian

Berengarius Carpensis — but why multiply names, every one of. which brings back the accession of a book which was an event almost like the birth of an infant?"

In 1833, before sailing for Europe to pursue his medical studies at the schools and hospitals of Paris, Holmes, in company with John Osborne Sargent and Park Benjamin, put out a little volume called "The Harbinger — a May Gift, dedicated to the ladies who have so kindly aided the New England Institution for the Education of the Blind." The collection was made at the suggestion of Dr. Samuel G. Howe, and was for sale at the fair for the blind got up in Faneuil Hall under the auspices of Mrs. Harrison Gray Otis, one of the most brilliant leaders of society in her day. "The Harbinger" contains five or six of the poems of Holmes that had elsewhere been published, including "The Ballad of the Oysterman."

From April, 1833, to October, 1835, Holmes was in Europe, most of the time in Paris, following various courses at the École de Médecine, and at various hospitals, especially at La Pitié with M. Louis. There are hints here and there in his writings of the two years in Europe, and of his gay but not dissipated life in Paris. He made *le grand tour*, but was too young to derive such benefit from the art and life of Europe as he would have received later in life, when more deeply versed in the history and literature of the Continent and of Great Britain. Boston is the most purely English of American cities, and Holmes, like a true Englishman, remained loyal, while abroad, to the kindred points of heaven and home. He has never taken so enthusiastically to objective humanitarian culture (art, ethnology, history, etc.) as he has to technical science and to the study of the human mind and character at first hand. Boston is his idol, to Boston he has addressed all his writings, and Boston it would seem he carried with him to Europe.

In August, 1836, after his return from abroad, Holmes read before the Phi Beta Kappa Society his long poem in rhymed heroics, styled "Poetry, a Metrical Essay," and designed to express some general truths on the sources and the machinery of poetry. It was the first of many read before the same society:—

"Scenes of my youth! awake its slumbering fire!
Ye winds of Memory, sweep the silent lyre!

   .   .   .   .   .

Long have I wandered; the returning tide
Brought back an exile to his cradle's side;
And as my bark her time-worn flag unrolled,
To greet the land-breeze with its faded fold,
So, in remembrance of my boyhood's time,
I lift these ensigns of neglected rhyme;
O more than blest, that, all my wanderings
     through,
My anchor falls where first my pennons flew!"

Mr. George Ticknor Curtis has spoken of the delivery of the poem to this effect:—

"Dr. Holmes had then just returned from Europe. Extremely youthful in his appearance, bubbling over with the mingled humor and pathos that have always marked his poetry, and sparkling with coruscations of his peculiar genius, his Phi Beta Kappa poem of 1836, delivered with a clear, ringing enunciation, which imparted to the hearers his own enjoyment of his thoughts and expressions, delighted a cultivated audience to a very uncommon degree."

A writer in the *American Monthly Maga-*

zine for 1837, p. 73 (probably Park Benjamin, one of the editors), also said : —

"A brilliant, airy, and *spirituelle* manner, varied with striking flexibility to the changing sentiment of the poem, — now deeply impassioned, now gayly joyous and nonchalant, and 'anon springing up almost into an actual flight of rhapsody, — rendered the delivery of this poem a rich, nearly a dramatic, entertainment, such as we have rarely witnessed. A grave, learned, and most intellectual discourse by Dr. Wayland of Brown University formed the solid part of this feast ; and when this had been finished, the cloth cleared, and the *entremets* of a little music had been discussed, on came the mellow wine, the ingenious, heterogeneous 'Trifle,' the fine-grained crystals of 'Ices,' and the golden fruit of a Dessert, in the shape of this beautiful poem."

In the same year Holmes published the first collection of his poems (Boston : Otis, Broaders & Co., 1836). The book includes forty-five poems and a preface of seven pages. The preface contains a defence of the extravagant, or hyperbolical, in poetry : —

"The *extravagant* is often condemned as

unnatural; as if a tendency of the mind, shown in all ages and forms, had not its foundation in nature. A series of hyperbolical images is considered beneath criticism by the same judges who would write treatises upon the sculptured satyrs and painted arabesques of antiquity, which are only hyperbole in stone and colors. As material objects in different lights repeat themselves in shadows variously elongated, contracted, or exaggerated, so our solid and sober thoughts caricature themselves in fantastic shapes inseparable from their originals, and having a unity in their extravagance which proves them to have retained their proportions in certain respects, however differing in outline from their prototypes."

We shall consider the poems of the volume in another chapter. But a little well-known anecdote about one of them is in point here. Abraham Lincoln, in conversation with some one, once said: "There are some quaint, queer verses, written, I think, by Oliver Wendell Holmes, entitled 'The Last Leaf,' one of which is to me inexpressibly touching." He then repeated the poem from memory, and as he finished this much admired stanza, —

> "The mossy marbles rest
>   On the lips that he has prest
>   In their bloom.
>   And the names he loved to hear
>   Have been carved for many a year
>   On the tomb," —

he said: "For pure pathos, in my judgment, there is nothing finer than those six lines in the English language." (See Appendix to Lamon's "Lincoln.") Poor Lincoln ! was he thinking of that lonely grave of his first love far away in Illinois? "Oh, I cannot endure the thought of her lying out there with the storms beating upon her," he said. There is nothing more touching in the annals of the heart than the overwhelming despair and actual and long-continued insanity of that noble mind over the death of the first idol of his soul.

It was in 1836 also that Holmes received his degree of M.D. from Harvard College, and we are therefore to think of him now as a young practising physician of Boston, his service in that capacity stretching over the years 1836–38 and 1840–47. It goes without saying that a young man with the finest medical education that the world could offer, related to "the first families" of Boston, engaging in manners, and popular with both sexes, would receive a warm welcome as a practitioner, and undoubtedly he could have built up a still greater practice than he did if he had not so soon entered upon the career of a college professor. As a practitioner he was, or eventually became, opposed to giving drugs in large quantities, unless in rare cases. His nature made it easy for him to enter a sick-room with a bright, cheerful countenance so as to inspire hope in the patient's mind. In his writings we get hints, here and there, of his working maxims, one of which, for example, was this : " When visiting a patient, enter the sick-room at once without keeping the patient in the torture of suspense by discussing the case with others in another room."

Boston, then a place of about sixty-five thousand inhabitants, had still somewhat of a semi-rural air with its quiet streets, old lawns and mansions, and stretches of green landscape westward from the city's side. The literary centre was the Old Corner Bookstore on Washington Street, and the young lions of the day were George Ticknor, Edward Everett, Daniel Webster, Sumner, Howe, Phillips, and others. Holmes met all these in society, as well as most of the Tories of Beacon Street, for whose company he has always had a fondness, or weakness. During the years 1835, 1836, and 1837 he was in the habit of spending many pleasant hours with Motley at the house of Park Benjamin, No. 14 Temple Place. Benjamin had been an old college friend, and they were received with the greatest cordiality. The curious antiquary who turns over the leaves of the old *Knickerbocker* magazines will find there many poems by Benjamin. His two sisters, at the time of which we are speaking, were in the bloom of young womanhood, and of course were the cynosure that had attracted the young men. Mary Benjamin became eventually the wife of Motley, and her sister married Motley's intimate friend, Mr. J. L. Stackpole.

In 1803 Ward Nicholas Boylston established in Boston a fund, the income of which was to be expended in prizes for medical dissertations. In 1836–37 the prizes were two medals worth fifty dollars each. Dr. Holmes gained these and one more, making three out of the four offered in two successive years. These "Boylston Prize Dissertations," which were published in book form in 1838, are fine scholarly essays, showing thoroughness of research on the inductive method. Their value is shown by the fact that in 1881, forty-three years after their publication, the editor of the *Boston Medical and Surgical Journal* advised his readers to peruse Dr. Holmes' Boylston Prize Essay on Intermittent Fever, the disease having recently reappeared. The essay is also very freely quoted in Dr. Adams' paper on intermittent fever, published in the 1881 report of the Health Department of the Massachusetts Board of Health, Lunacy, and Charity.

In 1838 Dr. Holmes was appointed Professor of Anatomy and Physiology in Dartmouth College, New Hampshire. He filled this position for two years, having for associate professors in the Medical Faculty Elisha

Bartlett, John Delamater, Oliver P. Hubbard, Dixi Crosby, and Stephen W. Williams.

After resigning his position at Dartmouth, Dr. Holmes returned to Boston, and on the 16th of June, 1840, was united in marriage to Miss Amelia Lee Jackson, daughter of the Hon. Charles Jackson, an eminent jurist and judge of the Massachusetts Supreme Court from 1813 to 1824. Judge Charles Jackson was a brother of Dr. James Jackson, the eminent medical author, and professor in the Harvard Medical School for many years.

The first residence of Holmes after his marriage was at No. 8 Montgomery Place, Boston, a little court leading out of Tremont Street, near Bromfield Street. In that house (at the left-hand side next the farther corner) he lived for nearly twenty years. " When he entered that door, two shadows glided over the threshold; five lingered in the doorway when he passed through it for the last time, — and one of the shadows was claimed by its owner to be longer than his own. What changes he saw in that quiet place! Death rained through every roof but his; children came into life, grew into maturity, wedded, faded away, threw themselves away; the whole drama of life was played in that stock-company's theatre of a dozen houses, one of which was his, and no deep sorrow or severe calamity ever entered his dwelling. Peace be to those walls, forever, — the Professor said, — for the many pleasant years he has passed within them ! "

The three children born to Dr. Holmes in Montgomery Place were Oliver Wendell (born 1841), Amelia Jackson, and Edward. The daughter is now Mrs. John Turner Sargent, and it is at her house in Beverly Farms, near Boston, that Professor Holmes has passed his summers for a number of years. Mr. Oliver Wendell Holmes, Jr., and Mr. Edward Holmes are both lawyers, — the former well-known for his legal writings, and withal so much of a public character, and so beloved by a wide circle of friends for sterling quali-ties of mind and heart, that one may be par-doned a few references to his life and work.

He studied as a boy in Boston at the school of Mr. E. S. Dixwell, whose daughter, Miss Fanny Dixwell, he afterwards married. In April, 1861, the year of his graduation from Harvard College, he joined the Fourth Battalion of Infantry, Major Thomas G. Stevenson, then at Fort Independence, Boston Harbor, where he wrote the poem for Class Day. He was wounded in the breast in the battle of Ball's Bluff,* and received a wound in the neck at Antietam, September 17, 1862, while acting as captain of Company G. In the *Atlantic Monthly* for 1862 (p. 738) Dr. Holmes has given a lively account of his " Hunt after the Captain " on this occasion, and of his journey to and from the battle-field. The piece is also included in Dr. Holmes' " Soundings from the Atlantic." We could ill have spared such an artless and feeling chapter in the history of parental love as that paper forms. The yearning of parental affection, delicately revealed in those pages, is a better testimony to the tender and beautiful emotional nature of the poet than the encomiums of a thousand friends would be. On his recovery Captain Holmes entered the service again, and received the commission of Lieutenant-Colonel, but was not mustered in (the

* See T. W. Higginson's Harvard Memorial Biographies, Vol. II. p. 478.

regiment being too much reduced), and served as aide-de-camp to Brigadier-General H. G. Wright, during General Grant's campaign of 1864. In 1866 he received the degree of LL.B. from Harvard University, and became a practising lawyer in Boston. He has taught and lectured on Constitutional Law and Jurisprudence in Harvard College. He had at one time editorial charge of the *American Law Review*. To the editing of Chancellor James Kent's "Commentaries on American Law" (Boston : Little, Brown, & Co., 1873, 4 vols.), he devoted three years of steady labor, and produced an edition of Kent which was received with the highest praise by jurists and lawyers. He has also published "The Common Law," and written, among other papers, the biography of A. Dehon in the Harvard Memorial Biographies. In 1882 Mr. Holmes was appointed Professor in the Harvard Law School, and served in that capacity for some weeks, when he resigned to accept an appointment as Justice in the Supreme Court of Massachusetts.

The career of Dr. Holmes as a practising physician drew to a close in the latter part of

1847, when he accepted an invitation to fill the chair of Anatomy and Physiology in the Harvard Medical School, a position which he held in unbroken continuity from that date up to the autumn of the year 1882, — a period of thirty-five years. He continued for two years after his appointment to act as a physician, but in 1849 gave up general practice altogether. Of his introductory lecture, delivered before the medical students, the *Boston Medical and Surgical Journal* (December, 1847) said : " The high expectations in regard to the new Professor of Anatomy in Harvard University have not been disappointed. His introductory lecture is the best discourse ever delivered in the Medical School of Harvard University." It is a singular circumstance, by the way, that only three persons in a century have held the chair recently vacated by Professor Holmes, — namely, Dr. John Warren, his son, John Collins Warren, and, lastly, Dr. Holmes. For many years Holmes delivered four lectures each week during the college year. Early in the administration of President Eliot the system of instruction was expanded by the division of the Parkman professorship into the chair of Anatomy and the chair of Physiology, Professor Holmes retaining the former.

The Medical School was removed to its present site at the foot of North Grove Street in 1846. It is not an inviting locality, and the interior of the building has a dilapidated, neglected, "old particular, brandy-punchy" appearance. The anatomical lecture-room is a deep pit, looking something like a ship's cabin (barring the amphitheatre of seats). There is a skylight, there are anatomical charts, and skeletons dangling from frames. The present writer attended one of the last recitations held by Professor Holmes in this room. As the instructor entered he was received with applause, — proof sufficient of his popularity. The tone of feeling manifested by the students was one of mingled respect, affection, and subdued gayety, — a state of titillation which might explode at any moment in a laugh ; and be sure that laughs were not infrequent at every lecture or recitation. After examining and testing two prepared specimens of nerve-fibre and nerve-cell, the Professor passed them around for inspection, they having been mounted in two of the convenient microscopes (with lamp attachment) devised by himself for class use. While the microscopes are passing around, the human scapula, or shoulder-bone, is taken up and questions asked about it in quick, decisive tones. At the anatomical blunders of the young saw-bones a laugh goes round ; the eyes of the doctor twinkle, and a kindly, mirth-provoking expression lights up his whole face while he looks not always at, but away from the student whom he is questioning : —

Professor. — " Smith ! Here take the bone ! What is the reason that the thigh-socket is so much deeper than the arm-socket ? "

Student does not seem clear on the point.

Professor. — " Because upon the leg rests the entire weight of the body, and it does not need much range of movement ; but the arm requires to be moved in every direction, as, for example, in knocking a man down, thus, or in the oratorical gesture " (both gestures being gracefully exemplified).

A general and hearty laugh by the class ensues, and the bone is passed on to the next man.

Dr. Holmes' instruction was usually given in the shape of extemporaneous lectures, illustrated by diagrams, microscopical preparations, models, etc. In some cases written lectures were prepared by him. For the purpose of making the young men acquainted with nature at first hand, he provided for them ten skeletons, each of which was divided into six parts, placed in boxes with handles and sliding covers. By taking these boxes to his room the student was enabled to study osteology to the best effect, *i. e.*, by actual handling of the objects studied.

Speaking at a certain anniversary meeting of Dr. Holmes' power as a specialist, President Eliot, of Harvard, said: —

"Most of you have perhaps the impression that Dr. Holmes chiefly enjoys a beautiful couplet, a beautiful verse, an elegant sentence. It has fallen to me to observe that he has other great enjoyments. I never heard any mortal exhibit such enthusiasm over an elegant dissection. . . . It is his to know with absolute precision the form of every bone in this wonderful body of ours, the course of every artery and vein, of every nerve, the form and function of every muscle, and not only to know it, but to describe it with a fascinating precision and enthusiasm."

By way of pleasant relief and contrast to urban matters, we are now to turn our attention to the enchanting Berkshire region, the " Switzerland of New England," where, in his Pittsfield residence of Canoe Place (so called by him in allusion to the mark on the ancient Indian deed of the estate), Dr. Holmes passed seven happy summer vacations, which, he says, stand in his memory like seven golden candlesticks seen in the beatific vision of the holy dreamer. His Pittsfield farm inured to Dr. Holmes through his mother, whose grandfather, Jacob Wendell, bought, in 1735, the entire township of Pontoosuc, containing twenty-four thousand acres. From the house a noble prospect was to be seen, including the winding river below and the distant hills and mountains. Near neighbors of the poet were the traveller and novelist, Herman Melville, and the novelist, G. P. R. James; not far to the south, in the Lenox region, were Miss Sedgwick and Miss Fanny Kemble, and

also, for a short time, Hawthorne. The praises
of the Berkshire region have often been sung
and spoken, and will be so spoken and sung
as long as the sentiment of beauty exists in
human minds : a height of twelve hundred
feet above the sea ; no mosquitoes ; air pure
and cool as "frozen dew poured from a silver
vase"; the sun-garden of the titanic azure
hills, far billowing; the sod-plush of the
mountains a tangle of hardy flowers and
beautiful wayside weeds and crispy sedge and
moss; the gold-vapor of sunset topping the
soft, distant violet and indigo tints of the
hills ; the wine-colored brooks humming old
tunes and flashing white curls to the sun as
they hurry down the mountain sides (Oh, the
joyous Arcadian life of those pastoral mountains !) ; the huckleberry pastures, inter-
sprinkled with sweet-scented bayberry and
the high-bush blackberry; the barberries
with their "bright-red coral pendants"; the
steeple-top, pussy-willow, yarrow, tanzy, the
white-flowered indian sage, the yellow ele-
campane, mouse-ear, crane-bill, gentian, wild
caraway, sweet fern, mountain mint; and,
in the woods, white scented violets, the

dark-stemmed maiden-hair, the swamp cabbage, birches, alders, hemlocks, and maples. A vast table-land of dim-blue hills, hung out in immensity like an exhalation or a dream, — this is the poetical view of it. A mighty fine milk country, — the practical view. By the way, we had almost forgotten to pay our respects to those arbutus flowers of Berkshire, — the Goodale sisters of South Egremont. Miss Elaine's pretty "Journal of a Farmer's Daughter". will help to fill out the picture of Berkshire scenery for those who are interested therein.

In 1852 Dr. Holmes delivered, in various cities, a course of lectures on the "English Poets of the Nineteenth Century," — Wordsworth, Moore, Keats, Shelley, and others.

"The style," says Duyckinck, "was precise and animated; the illustrations sharp and cleanly cut. In the criticism there was a leaning rather to the bold and dashing bravura of Scott and Byron than to the calm, philosophical mood of Wordsworth. Where there was any game on the wing, when the 'servile herd' of imitators and poetasters came in view, they were dropped at once by a felicitous shot. Each lecture closed with a copy of verses, humorous or sentimental, growing out of the prevalent mood of the hour's discussion."

As a lecturer Holmes was much in demand, and for a half-dozen years or so he travelled a great deal in this capacity. The reader will find some humorous remarks on the subject in the "Autocrat."

About the year 1856 Dr. Holmes thus defined his lecturing terms in a letter to a certain official : —

"My terms for a lecture, when I stay over night, are fifteen dollars and expenses, a room with a fire in it, in a public house, and a mattress to sleep on, — not a feather-bed. As you write in your individual capacity, I tell you at once all my habitual exigencies. I am afraid to sleep in a cold room ; I can't sleep on a feather-bed ; I will not go to private houses ; and I have fixed upon the sum mentioned as what it is worth for me to go away for the night to places that cannot pay more."

Fifteen dollars !

The Autocrat's landlady, too, delivers herself as follows on this subject : —

"He was a man that loved to stick round home as much as any cat you ever see in your life. He used to say he'd as lief have a tooth pulled as go away anywheres. Always got sick, he said, when he went away, and never sick when he didn't. Pretty nigh killed himself goin' about lecterin' two or three winters, —talkin' in cold country lyceums,—as he used to say, — goin' home to cold parlors and bein' treated to cold apples and cold water; and then goin' up into a cold bed in a cold chamber, and comin' home next mornin' with a cold in his head as bad as the horse distemper. Then he'd look kind of sorry for havin' said it, and tell how kind some of the good women was to him, — how one spread an edderdown comforter for him, and another fixed up somethin' hot for him after the lecter, and another one said, 'There now, you smoke that cigar of yours after the lecter just as if you was at home,' — and if they'd all been like that, he'd have gone on lecterin' forever, but as it was, he got pooty nigh enough of it, and preferred nateral death to puttin' himself out of the world by such violent means as lecterin.''

CHAPTER V.

THE AUTOCRAT OF THE BREAKFAST-TABLE.

Boston, — city of the brown loaf, and the
marrow-searching icy winds ; city of the brave
heart and powerful hand; city beloved of
freedom,

> "Hic illius arma,
> Hic currus ; "

city whirling through space with bright golden
dome and streaming starry flags ;

> "Peace, Freedom, Wealth ! no fairer view,
> Though with the wild bird's restless wings
> We sailed beneath the noontide's blue
> Or chased the moonlight's endless rings ! "
>
> — *Holmes.*

What Addison and Steele were to the Lon-
don of their day ; what Lamb and Hazlitt
were to the same city at a later date ; what
De Quincey, North, and Jeffrey were to dun
Edin of Scotland, — that Holmes and the
Atlantic Monthly coterie of a quarter of a cen-

tury ago were to Boston. The streets of London were not more loved by Johnson and Lamb than those of Boston have been by Holmes. A perfect thing in its kind is always admirable. Hence to the autocrat and laureate of Boston, to Holmes the consummate, the most perfect and delightful oppidan, richest distillation of the old Puritan strain of blood, master at will of smiles or tears, — to him we are constrained to yield our homage. He has only made short swallow-flights beyond the limits of his beloved city. If he goes to Paris, he carries Boston with him; if he goes to New York or Philadelphia, he only sighs and compares them with Boston to their disadvantage, and gets back as quick as he can to the hub of the solar system. A barnacle is not more closely identified with its rock, or a pearl with its oyster, than Holmes is with St. Botolph's town. All his books might be labelled " Talks with my Neighbors," and this very provincialism, or urban patriotism, forms their chief charm.

What then is Boston? What is the typical New Englander? He is above all things a person of almost pure and unmixed English blood; he is a proud English squire, unmellowed, exacerbated, and æstheticized by change of climate; for juicy mutton, split codfish; for the delicate and soothing air of the Gulf Stream, the icy winds of Labrador; for the sweet hawthorn hedge, the boulder fence; for fat haunches of turf peppered with buttercups and daisies, a soil that scarcely hides the granite. The Bostonian is simply an Americanized Englishman. Hence his hauteur and gigantic egotism. As the Englishman is the physical bully of the world, so the Bostonian is the æsthetic and intellectual bully of America; underneath the high polish of consummate manners (the Pheidian faces finished with a hair-pencil, the animal faultlessly encased) there lurk the stony glare of self-aggrandizement, the icy complacency of ancestral pride (*odi profanum vulgus*), the *de haut en bas* air of an intellectual and social aristocracy well ballasted by the weighty annals of the past. Boston idealizes itself in its artists' *atéliers*, enjoys artificial æsthetic aspiration in its wealthy ecclesiastical clubs, sublimates its emotions in Music

Hall, martyrs its comfort with the arid inanities of drawing-room receptions, speculates in its granite exchanges, intellectualizes New England with its pale cast of thought, and, in the intervals, subjects the universe in general to the remorseless inspection of its critical eye-glass.

Ten years of refrigeration and camphoration, two lustrums of severe study, are hardly too much for you, O sunny-hearted child of the South or West, if you would hope to pass unscathed the gauntlet of eyes, and move unterrified in the social circles of the Puritan capital. But be sure to persevere; beware of a precipitate judgment and flight; for you will soon find that "the old red-running blood" is in the arteries of the New Englander too, the old warm human heart and tender compassion. Only wait, and you shall find yourself possessed of a warm affection for the gallant city, solidly seated there on its storied hill, — distinguished in its manners, profuse in its philanthropies, splendid in its patriotism, and a model of excellence in its highly organized corporate life. In what other American city as yet is materiality, the grossness of life, properly subordinated to the intellectual or ideal ? Look, *e. g.*, at these blooming young women and these silver-haired matrons coming out of one of their clubs on Park Street ; observe the mingling of graciousness and French *délicatesse* of manners with austere sweetness, firm will, transparent innocence, and energetic carriage and action ; outwardly, snow and roses on a porcelain vase ; inwardly, aflame with ideal aspiration, and busied with noble charities and humanitarian reforms. There are plenty of European cities dominated even more than Boston by the spirit of idealism ; but there is no other spot on the globe where women hold so high a position ;—and the status of woman in a society is the most delicate test of its civilization.

In the midst of this homogeneous and cultured community the *Atlantic Monthly* magazine one day, in November, 1857, spread out a literary feast,* and at the head of its table

---

* In the same number of the magazine, and just preceding the first instalment of the " Autocrat," appeared a cluster of Emerson's philosophical poems, including the famous " Brahma."

appeared one of the most brilliant and versatile conversationalists of modern times, — the Autocrat of the Breakfast-Table, one who "invented a new kind in literature," — a combination of poetry, psychical introspection, and practical philosophy, irradiated by delicate wit, gay humor, and irresistible drollery. A periodical magazine is just the kind of medium suited to a conversationalist. He is sure of a wide group of sympathetic listeners, whom he can address in a familiar, colloquial style, and have his words reach them while still warm from his lips. The "Autocrat" papers created a lively sensation. "The reader of the *Atlantic*," says Mr. Francis H. Underwood, "always turned to the 'Autocrat' first. This was proven after the first number by the notices of the press. Very odd most of the early notices were. The good, sedate critics did not know what to make of the thing. Some thought it undignified. Others professed to be more confirmed in their opinion that Holmes was only an inordinate egotist. The suckling reviewer undertook to put the puns under his microscope for analysis. The solemn purist lamented the tendency to slang ; and while he admitted the brilliancy of the poems that were interspersed, he thought they showed as ill as diamonds among the spangles of the court fool."

But before discussing the "Autocrat" papers any further let us recall the circumstances connected with the founding of the *Atlantic Monthly.* Its establishment was due to the then vigorous publishing firm of Phillips & Sampson. Mr. Phillips was especially active and sanguine in promoting the enterprise. One of the objects of the magazine was to give aid and countenance to the anti-slavery cause. The financial outlook at that time was hardly such as to promise success to the new enterprise, and the wiseacres shook their heads over it, foreboding its early collapse. And in truth it did have a hard struggle for existence, and many thousand dollars of capital were thrown overboard in the effort to keep the ship afloat. It is thought that but for the *prestige* which the "Autocrat" papers gave, the concern would inevitably have gone to pieces.

The first editor was James Russell Lowell,

who was nominated by Mr. Francis H. Underwood. Mr. Lowell thought that Dr. Holmes
would have been the better choice, and expressed the conviction that he (Holmes)
would do great things, and make himself felt
as a new force in literature. This well-
fufilled prediction must have been chiefly
based on Mr. Lowell's acquaintance with the
rich and brilliant conversation and poetry of
Holmes, for he had as yet done nothing great
in the way of prose, with the exception of his
(still unpublished) Lectures on the " English
Poets of the Nineteenth Century," which
were first delivered before the Lowell Institute in Boston in 1852.

The name of the magazine was suggested
by Dr. Holmes. The founders, or first corps
of contributors, included Longfellow, Emerson, Holmes, Motley, Charles Eliot Norton,
Edmund Quincy, J. Elliot Cabot, Francis H.
Underwood, and others, — fourteen in all.
According to a statement of one of the founders, the magazine was born in Cambridge
at Porter's Tavern on North Avenue, an
old inn famous for its *cuisine* and its punch
since half a century. Not that our staid Puri-

tan divines and essayists ever indulged in such drinking as did their predecessors at Ambrose's in Gabriel's Road. But be sure that "the old man of the lion heart and the sceptre crutch" (Kit North), supported by Ensign Odoherty and the Ettrick Shepherd, never delivered a steadier fire of crackling jests than shot back and forth over the glittering table at Porter's or at Parker's when such wits as Holmes and Lowell sat opposite to each other : —

> " Such jests, that, drained of every joke,
> The very bank of language broke, —
> Such deeds that Laughter nearly died
> With stitches in his belted side ;
> While Time, caught fast in pleasure's chain,
> His double goblet snapped in twain,
> And stood with half in either hand, —
> Both brimming full, — but not of sand ! "
>
> — *Holmes.*

To Mr. F. H. Underwood in *Scribner's Magazine* we are indebted for the following brilliant bit of reminiscence of these early *Atlantic* dinners, associated with the founding and first days of the magazine : " The sparkle of the after-dinner talk was incommunicable, —

not in the least studied, but natural and exuberant. The absolute loss of those conversations and encounters of wit, when Emerson, Longfellow, Holmes, Lowell, and others sat about the board, is greatly to be regretted. Judge Hoar, who inherits the wit of Roger Sherman, bore his full part. Lowell probably uttered more elaborate sentences, — glowing with new-born images; Holmes made the simplest play and scored most points, both serious and comic. Meanwhile Emerson's wise face was lighted by a miraculous smile that would have been the delight and despair of a painter; and in the end he took the thought which the others were playing hocky with, and calmly set it in an apothegm of crystal beauty.

"The 'Atlantic' Club at times was ambulatory, although it generally met at Parker's. Once or twice it dined at Point Shirley with Taft, who is *facile rex* of our sea-board. Once it dined at a little restaurant in Winter Place, kept by a man of versatile genius, M. Fontarive, the first of the French cooks of the time. Once it met at Zach. Porter's in North Cambridge, — not a hotel, but an old-fashioned tavern.   The cooking was marvellous, and was done under the landlord's eye.   His creed was that of Ezra Weeks of the Eagle Inn : —

" ' Nothin' riles me, I pledge my fastin' word,
    Like cookin' out the natur' of a bird.'

"The ducks were brought in and carved by Porter himself, as a mark of consideration to the distinguished guests.   The knife was keen, and was wielded by a deft hand ; the slices fell about the platter like a mower's swath until the carcass was bare as a barrel.

" 'What do you do with the bird after that ? ' Lowell asked of the landlord.

" 'Wal,' said Porter, with a curious twinkle in his eyes, 'when I've sliced off the breast, an' the wings, an' legs like that' (pointing to the shell), 'I gin'rally give the carkess to the poor.'

"Dr. Palmer, whose East Indian sketches had just been published and greatly admired, was a special guest on this occasion; and the fun of the chorus of palanquin bearers was as current about the table as 'Pinafore' phrases to-day.   Holmes was in high spirits, and talked his best, mostly to Longfellow.   It was almost like a veritable autocrat in full activity, coruscating, punning, and bearing all before him.'

"There were no horse-cars then, I think, or it might have been late ; at all events, the whole party, including Emerson, Longfellow, and the other Olympians, walked down to Harvard Square through nearly a foot of new-fallen snow. The impression of this intellectual feast is ineffaceable, but it seems now as far away as the Trojan war."

The Dr. Palmer alluded to by Mr. Underwood was Dr. John Williamson Palmer, who in 1852-53 had served through the Burmese campaign as surgeon in one of the East India Company's war steamers, and had travelled a good deal in India. His Oriental papers in the first numbers of the *Atlantic* are full of the most rollicking fun. (See Appendix I.)

Another organization which brought together many of the contributors to the *Atlantic* was the Saturday Club, which met, and still meets, every Saturday at two o'clock in the mirror-room at Parker's. Members in the early days were Felton, Whipple, Judge Hoar, James Freeman Clarke, Agassiz, and others. It has owed its longevity to its entire informality, and its freedom from speech-making.

To return to the " Autocrat of the Breakfast-Table." The original, or prototypal, papers published under this title in Buckingham's *New England Magazine* for 1831 and 1832, were written by Holmes while a law-student in Cambridge, and are indeed boyish and uncombed literary productions, although the searching glance may detect in them the germ or crude hint of every characteristic of the " Autocrat " of 1857. They consist of detached paragraphs,—fragmentary and un-related aphoristic remarks on all manner of subjects. We must respect the wisdom that led their author to deprecate a resurrection of these early pieces. Their coarse slang, egot-ism, flippancy, and priggishness are scarcely redeemed by the few gems that glitter here and there, giving promise of the genial writer into which the boy of twenty-two was to develop in after years. Yet, in spite of the rawness and unabashed sophomorism of the style, one feels, in reading these early trial chapters, that pleasant excitation which decided originality always produces. In this respect, but in no other, they are superior to Longfellow's articles styled "The Schoolmaster," published in the same numbers of the magazine. The following whimsical stanzas appear in Buckingham's magazine, and have not been republished by Dr. Holmes; but they are so good that he will doubtless pardon their reproduction :—

"TO A LADY WITH HER BACK TO ME.

(Written while sailing up the Delaware.)

"I know thy face is fresh and bright,
　Thou angel-moulded girl ;
I caught one glimpse of purest white,
　I saw one auburn curl.

"O would the whispering ripples breathe
　The thoughts that vainly strive —
She turns — she turns to look on me ;
　Black ! cross-eyed ! seventy-five !"

There are two or three prose bits in the first "Autocrat" papers worth quoting, — as these :—

"There is a dilute atmosphere of learning which extends to some distance around a literary institution, almost as bad as the vacuum of ignorance.   Within such precincts I would look for the Flat in his most spiritless inanity, and the Bore at the acme of intensity."

"Drink as much as you please before your grandfather, but mind whom you kiss before your little brother."

Here is a powerful psychological delineation of a murderer's soul : —

" His eye, as nearly as I could tell of a misty-gray, was fixed and calm, but it seemed to convey no more perception to his mind than if he had been talking to a phantom. When the springs that supply the soul are all cut off, for a little while, her dark waters heave vainly against their barriers, and then hush themselves into stillness and blackness. A few hidden fountains may break up and pour themselves into her bosom ; but day by day her circle is narrowing, and the depths, once covered, lie bare in their desolation."

It is hardly necessary to state that the early " Autocrat " papers gave only their title to the later ones of 1857.   In the twenty-five years that had passed, the entire diapason of manhood had been played over, and the most that life has to offer of joy or sorrow had been tasted. The pent-up thoughts of this long period — all its observations and experiences — are now (in 1857) flung out upon the page in the light and airy form of breakfast-table chat. The charm is in the spontaneity. "Remembering," says Holmes, "some crude papers of mine in an old magazine, it occurred to me that their title might serve for some pert papers, and so I sat down and wrote off what came into my head under the title, 'The Autocrat of the Breakfast-Table.' This work was not the result of an express premeditation, but was, as I may say, dipped from the running stream of my thoughts."

As in actual life our pleasantest hours are those intensified periods passed at table in social converse, so in these papers we have a vigorous and sustained creation of thoughts and feelings and table-chat so true to the life (the conversational part of it) as to seem like an actual short-hand report. The "Autocrat" is packed full of sententious practical knowl-edge, nut-shell sayings, polished gems of thought, flashes of wit, and keen and sub-tle *aperçus* into the foibles and idiosyn-crasies of men and women. It is glowing poetry in a prose dress (there are poems too); it is the rich liquor of experience decanted from its darkling receptacle into the sheen and sparkle of cut-glass. There is nothing in literature with which it can be compared unless it be the "Noctes Ambrosianæ" of Professor Wilson; and it has a clearer, more delicate ring than that work, although not so grand-hearted and tumultuous and self-forgetful. It is a book, said an English critic,* "to conjure up a cosey winter-picture, of a ruddy fire, and singing kettle, soft hearth-rug, warm slippers, and easy chair; a musical chime of cups and saucers, fragrance of tea and toast within : and those flowers of frost fading on the windows without, as though old winter just looked in, but his cold breath was melted, and so he passed by. A book to possess two copies of; one to be read and marked, thumbed and dog-eared; and one to stand up in its pride of place with the rest on the shelves, all ranged in shining rows, as dear old friends, and not merely as nodding acquaintances."

One of the features of the book is its ren-

* In the *North British Review* for November, 1860.

dering of those subtle and elusive thoughts that are rarely put into words ; as that about the sensation we so often experience of having done or thought something similar or identical before, and in similar circumstances, and of having had this feeling in dreams also ; or that remark about the tendency we have to string adjectives or epithets in triads, and the explanation offered that " it is an instinctive and involuntary effort of the mind to present a thought or image with the three dimensions that belong to every solid."

To all the pleasant interpretations of our unspoken thought in the " Autocrat " we keep saying, in the words of the old gentleman who sat at the landlady's table, " That's it ! that's it !" as when we read that the thing that more than anything else spoils good conversation consists of " long arguments on special points between people who differ on the fundamental principles on which these points depend "; or when the Autocrat announces that he allows no bullying facts at this table, and remarks that the fluent harmonies of conversation may be spoiled by the intrusion of a single false note ; or when he says that the work of logic is, generally speaking, to build a *pons asinorum* over chasms which shrewd people can bestride without such a structure; or when London on Derby day is likened to a shelled corn-cob, "and there is not a clerk who could raise the money to hire a saddle with an old hack under it that can sit down on his office-stool the next day without wincing."

There are one or two sayings in the "Autocrat" that have become proverbial ; namely, the remark that the finest specimens of the New England character are raised under glass ; and the *mot* which gives to Boston the title "hub of the solar system" (not "hub of the universe," as it is sometimes quoted).* The poems included in the volume are, as a body, the author's very best, — "The Chambered Nautilus," "Latter-Day Warnings," "Æstivation," "The One-Hoss Shay," "Ode

* The Hon. George Folsom, in his Life of Sir Ferdinando Gorges, quotes a certain querulous agent of the Plymouth Colony to this effect. "All the frame of heaven moves upon one axis, and the whole of New England's interest seems designed to be loaden on one bottom, and her particular motions to be concentric to the Massachusetts tropic."

for a Social Meeting, with slight Alterations by a Teetotaller," etc. There are a few slight deficiencies in the "Autocrat." The poems are introduced a little awkwardly, and the machinery of the characters and of the boarding-house is a little tiresome, and in the succeeding volumes of the "Professor" and the "Poet" becomes unspeakably wearisome. In the latter volumes the poor straw-men, or lay-figures, set up for the author to exercise his wit upon, get completely worn out with being so long buffeted about, poor things! The straw sticks out at their elbows, and the sawdust dribbles from their armpits, until, like Don Quixote at Master Peter's Puppet-Show, we would fain, in our impatience, fall upon the whole rabble rout and hustle them out of our sight. But in the "Autocrat" proper these characters — the Schoolmistress, Benjamin Franklin, the Landlady, etc., — are pretty skilfully subordinated to the chief actor, or talker, in the scene, and, as a whole, the work is justly ranked with such productions as Emerson's "Conduct of Life" or Lamb's "Essays of Elia."

Narrow and acrid, indeed, must be the

nature that would find fault with Dr. Holmes'
chief work because it is mainly monologue.
Shall not the Autocrat wield his sceptre?
Grant that —

> "Though he changes dress and name,
> The man beneath is still the same,
> Laughing or sad, by fits and starts,
> One actor in a dozen parts,
> And whatsoe'er the mask may be,
> The voice assures us, *This is he.*"

Grant this, and say that this is not good
drama, still we are glad to have his thought
in any shape; and, regarding the "Autocrat"
alone, we say with its author that it is not
much matter, after all,

> "If the figures seen
> Are only shadows on a screen,
> He finds in them his lurking thought,
> And on their lips the words he sought,
> Like one who sits before the keys
> And plays a tune himself to please."

In 1882, twenty-five years after the penning of the "Autocrat," Dr. Holmes wrote
a new preface to the work, and added some

interesting foot-notes. He alluded to the great change that had taken place in the religious opinions of people, saying that when he wrote his Breakfast-Table series it almost meant social martyrdom to utter truths that can now be spoken and defended in any circle of listeners without offence.

CHAPTER VI.

In the Proceedings of the Massachusetts Historical Society for December, 1859, Dr. Holmes gives an agreeable account of a visit paid by him to Washington Irving in December, 1858, the year before Irving died : —

"Sunnyside was *snowyside* on that December morning; yet the thin white veil could not conceal the features of a place long familiar to me through the aid of engravings and photographs, and as stereotyped in the miraculous, solid sun-pictures. The sharp-pinnacled roof, surmounted by the old Dutch weather-cock; the vine-clad cottage, with its three-arched open porch, — open on all sides, like the master's heart, — were there just as I knew them, just as thousands know them who have never trodden or floated between the banks of the Hudson.

"We knocked and were admitted, feeling

still very doubtful whether Mr. Irving would be able to see us. Presently we heard a slow step, which could not be mistaken in that household of noiseless footfalls. Mr. Irving entered the room, and welcomed us in the most cordial manner. He was slighter and more delicately organized than I had supposed; of less than average stature, I should think, looking feeble, but with kindness beaming from every feature. He spoke almost in a whisper, with effort, his voice muffled by some obstruction. Age had treated him like a friend ; borrowing somewhat, as is his wont, but lending also those gentle graces which give an inexpressible charm to the converse of wise and good old men, whose sympathies keep their hearts young and their minds open. . . . Something authorized me to allude to his illness, and my old professional instincts led me to suggest to him the use of certain palliatives which I had known to be used in some cases having symptoms resembling his own.

"After returning home I sent him some articles of this kind. Early in January he wrote me a letter of considerable length ;

saying, among other things, that he had used some medicated *cigarettes* I sent him with much relief. This letter was overflowing with expressions of kindness; but, though written in his own hand, it had no signature. I sent it back to him for his name; telling him that his was the first autograph I had ever asked for, but that I must have it at the end of such a letter. The next post brought the letter back signed."

In 1858 Holmes removed from the old Montgomery Place home to 21 Charles Street, where he had as neighbors Governor Andrew and James T. Fields. His study, in the rear of the house, commanded a wide and beautiful view of Charles River, with the towns of Cambridge and Brighton, and the green slopes of Corey and Parker hills in the distance. Here twice a day, almost beneath the very windows, the tidal waters of the ocean come surging in along the sinuous Charles, bearing the perfume and strength of the sea in their arms. To the right one sees the long procession of travellers along West Boston bridge; in the distance loom the spires of Cambridge; the far-off hills are full of beauty, their tints ever changing; and at evening you have in full view

> " The gorgeous, indolent, sinking sun,
>   Burning, expanding the air."

At night there is something Venetian in the appearance of the Back Bay, as the expansion of the Charles River here is styled. The long lamp-rows of the bridges and of the Brighton road, the colored lights streaming down into the reflected abyss of the sky, the gleam of the smooth elastic surface of the stream, the expanse of stars, — it is all very soothing and beautiful of a summer evening. By day a prominent feature of the landscape is formed by the smoke-pillars from the tall East Cambridge factory-chimneys, — the giant-twisted smoke-columns of jet or snow, pinnacled in the azure sky, silent, sinuous, stately, the grace of motion and contour in perfect and harmonious expression. In winter the scene is still full of charm, with variety of tint and aspect, — the distant snow-line meeting that of the sky, the ships, the ice, the wheeling gulls, etc. From his study-window Dr. Holmes used to look out with an opera-glass at the little groups of tent-like screens made of sail-cloth and used by men who were fishing through the ice. There was then, and there is to-day, a good deal of fishing for eels and smelts from West Boston bridge. In the "Autocrat" Dr. Holmes tells us about his rowing experiences on the Charles and about the harbor. He kept several boats at the foot of his garden. *His* boat was the delicate "shell" with its antennæ-oars.

The "Autocrat of the Breakfast-Table" was followed in 1859 by "The Professor at the Breakfast-Table," a work distinctly inferior to its predecessor, but containing many fine single passages, and one episode, the "Story of Iris," which possesses great pathos and beauty, and has been reprinted in Rossiter Johnson's "Little Classics." The last moments of the poor old starved tutor, and his words to his little daughter, will draw the tears from the eyes of many a reader: "'Iris!' he said, — '*filiola mea!*' — The child knew this meant *my dear little daughter* as well as if it had been English. — 'Rainbow!' — for he would translate her name at times, — 'come to me, — *veni*' — and his lips went on automatically, and murmured, '*vel venito!*' — The child came and sat by his bedside, and took his hand, which she could not warm, but which shot its rays of cold all through her slender frame. But there she sat, looking steadily at him. Presently he opened his lips feebly, and whispered, '*Moribundus.*' She did not know what that meant, but she saw that there was something new and sad. So she began to cry; but presently remembering an old book that seemed to comfort him at times, got up and brought a Bible in the Latin version, called the Vulgate. 'Open it,' he said, — 'I will read, — *segnios irritant,* — don't put the light out, — ah! *haeret lateri,* — I am going, — *vale, vale, vale,* good-by, good-by — the Lord take care of my child! — *Domini audi,* — *vel audito!*' His face whitened suddenly, and he lay still, with open eyes and mouth. He had taken his last degree."

As a treasury of practical philosophy and observation, the " Professor " is a valuable and readable book; but as a story or narrative it is a failure. The everlasting boarders appear on the stage again, as lifeless and characterless as ever. The style is turgid, and frothy, and wearisome. Simplicity and the calmness of a great nature is what the reader comes to long for. The *Christian Examiner* said of "The Professor at the Breakfast-Table": "The anxiety to leave out nothing in the estimate of the universe, whether of old ideals or of new experiences, and the anxiety not to be too anxious, are curiously balanced throughout the book. There is a keen susceptibility to impressions, outward or inward, checked by the desire not to be led away by these impressions, and a belief that the base and issue of things are both good and right."

In the "Autocrat" Professor Holmes had expressed the opinion that every man has in him the material for one novel at least; for one's own life experiences would furnish him with such material. This hint of the inevitable novel, at which everybody nowadays tries his or her hand, took shape in 1859 in that weird New England story, "Elsie Venner, a Romance of Destiny," which exerted its subtle and thrilling fascination over a wide circle of readers, and was followed in 1867 by the somewhat similar novel, " The Guardian Angel."

Of the *technical* qualifications of the professional novel-wright Holmes has not wherewith to furnish forth even a third-rate genius ; there are twenty-and-one novelists now living who would laugh to scorn the threadbare conventionalisms of his plots, notwithstanding their few thrilling dramatic incidents. But then his two novels are not so much novels of plot as they are stories written to illustrate a psychological theory of heredity, and the interest chiefly centres, and was intended to centre, upon the one character in the novel whose nature and life experiences set forth the theory. The strength of " Elsie Venner " and " The Guardian Angel " lies in their shrewd psychological analysis of character (or rather of mental states), and in their wealth of practical philosophy, incidental information, and strong flavor of New Englandism. Certain types of New England character are sketched in coarse, raw pigments with great fidelity ; but, when the author is depicting his subordinate and ruder personages, you generally receive the impression of grotesque exaggeration and caricature (like that of firelight shadows on the wall). On such occasions he has an irresistible tendency to indulge in a kind of horse-play, a coarse realism of portraiture to a great extent lacking in the subtle and delicate touch by which the great novelists reveal the hidden springs of feeling and nobleness even in their least prominent characters. There is a certain harshness or hardness of manner in Dr. Holmes' novels. " Elsie Venner " and " The Guardian Angel" are pervaded throughout by a physiological atmosphere, with a whiff now and then from the peculiar medicated air of the physician's office. When Dr. Holmes brings a new character before us, or before himself, he is apt to begin his delineation with a sensuous, physiological study of the outward casing, tells us about the suits of muscles — the trapezius, the deltoid, the triceps — and many other facts of the kind.

The readers of Holmes who know that his chief trait is self-consciousness, and that the power of projecting himself into the lives of others, and becoming those others for a time, is something only with difficulty and effort accomplished by him, get the feeling that, in the character of novelist, he is only playing a *rôle*, — as if he had said, "Go to! I can write a novel as well as others; see in how approved a fashion I do it." A feature of his two novels which strengthens this impression is that many of their details seem not to have been premeditated, but to have been ground out as the writer went on.

But in spite of their deficiencies the stories hold us fascinated to the end. This means that they are successful works; and, indeed, they have had, and still have, a wide circle of readers. "Elsie Venner," especially, has attracted great attention on both sides of the Atlantic.

A few words should be said about our author's types of women, or let us say his typical woman. It is, perhaps, too much to expect that a physician and physiologist should have a very exalted idea of woman. We should hardly expect one who spends his life in considering the weak and diseased specimens of any group of nature's productions, to have a high ideal view of the present excellences and latent possibilities of development of the group as a sound and beautiful whole.   Dr. Holmes, at any rate, is half a century behind the times in his conception of woman.   His women are little more than pretty pieces of flesh, "fine specimens of muliebrity," "fine specimens of young females."   "The less there is of sex about a woman," he says, "the more she is to be dreaded."   There is of course a good deal of truth in this statement, and there is truth in Dr. Holmes' delineation of the womanly type as being at its best and highest (domestically speaking) when the softness and grace of wifehood and maternity are in normal and harmonious expression.   But what we quarrel with him for is that he stops there and shows himself apparently incapable of conceiving of woman in her relations outside of the domestic circle, where, equally with man outside of the relations of fatherhood and the home, she appears as an aspiring human being, athirst for knowledge and power and æsthetic enjoyment.   There is not apparently in all of Dr. Holmes' writings a single passage which expresses any sympathy with woman in her nobler ideal aspirations and struggles. Personally, he is popular with women, as most physicians are ; but he has been taken to task for his low ideal of womanhood by more than one female writer. Listen to him : "I confess I like the quality-ladies better than the common kind even of literary ones. They haven't read the last book, perhaps, but they attend better to you when you are talking to them. If they are never learned they make up for it in tact and elegance. Besides, I think, on the whole, there is less of self-assertion in diamonds than in dogmas." He has no doubt that Esther " was a more gracious and agreeable person than Deborah, who judged the people and wrote the story of Sisera." . . . "A woman who does not carry a halo of good feeling and desire to make everybody contented about with her wherever she goes, — an atmosphere of grace, mercy, and peace, of at least six feet radius, which wraps every human being upon whom she voluntarily bestows her presence, and so flatters him with the comfortable thought that she is rather glad he is alive than otherwise, isn't worth the trouble of talking to *as a woman;* she may do well enough to hold discussions with."

Observe the complacent masculine arrogance (so naïve !), the reference of the whole matter to one's self : the question with him is not whether woman shall develop herself nobly or not, but does she please *me,* does she flatter me, comfort me, and add to my enjoyment.   It is such seraglio philosophy as this that brings the sneer to the lips of the nobler women when they are discussing men among themselves.   But we may not be too harsh in our strictures.   For, although such philosophy as this is now happily almost entirely relegated to the less liberalized ranks of society, it was not so thirty or forty years ago ; the prevalent conception then was that which appears in the writings of Holmes.   He has of late both in print and in private conversation expressed the wish that he could recall many things written in his earlier years, and we shall doubtless be right in including among these certain pages or paragraphs in which he has treated of woman.   Let us not forget to add that his portraitures of the doll-type of women are very pretty and attractive. Iris, Myrtle Hazard, Olive Eveleth, Letty Forrester, — they are all charming little women, lovable and wifely. What a subtle conception that of Iris! Falling in love with the deformed Little Gentleman, and then, in the utter goodness and eternal womanly devotion of her soul, trying to idealize deformity, and look at it as one of Nature's eccentric curves, and a necessary part of the system of beauty; and then filling her drawing-book with creatures having twisted spines, humped dromedaries, high-shouldered herons, buffaloes, and twisted serpents! And her devotion in caring for the poor dwarf in his last illness, all this is very noble, and goes far toward making us pleased with Dr. Holmes' conception of woman as wife. Iris is indeed a delicate creature.

But the reader will get better hints of Dr. Holmes' methods as a novelist by examining with us the separate works. "Elsie Venner" appeared under the title of "The Professor's Story," in 1859 and 1860. The central conception of the novel is a weird and powerful one, strongly grasped and consistently and subtly elaborated in its details. One who is about to become a mother is bitten by a rattlesnake. The mother lives for three weeks after the birth of the child and then dies. The child, infected and serpentized by the poison, grows up, and manifests many of the characteristics of the snake. The story is a tragedy : poor serpentoid Elsie excites either pity or horror in all breasts but one, that of her old black nurse, Sophy, who really loves her. But her rich and passionate nature asks a deeper and more intimate love than this, and when she finds that the young scholar upon whom she has bestowed her affection cannot return it she dies in despair ; but love has acted as a spell to release her from the weird enchantment, and before she dies she seems completely free from the terrifying serpentine looks and actions which have characterized her, and leaves with us the impression that if she could only have had her love returned she would have been cured of her inherited taint, and would have had a happy married life.* This bringing back into

* Compare carefully pages 231 and 232 with page 262 (Vol. II., original edition).

human fellowship and sympathy of some abnormal or sin-scarred individual through the potent might of love, or the growth of human affection and sympathy, is also the central idea of "The Guardian Angel," of the "Silas Warner" of George Eliot, and of nearly all of Hawthorne's works, — only in Holmes' stories the taint is physiological ; in the others it is ethical. The isolation which was the lot of poor Elsie is described by Hawthorne in "The Marble Faun" as the "perception of an infinite shivering solitude, amid which we cannot come close enough to human beings to be warmed by them, and where they turn to cold, chilly shapes of mist." This isolation was the lot of Gervase Hastings, of Ethan Brand, of old Rappaccini, Hollingsworth, Roger Chillingsworth, Hester Prynne, and Donatello. When Hester forgot herself in ministrations to the suffering and sorrowing she lost the sense of her guilt, and "the scarlet letter ceased to be a stigma ;" in the case of Donatello, "when first the idea was suggested of living for the welfare of his fellow-creatures, the original beauty, which sorrow had partly effaced, came back elevated and spiritualized. In the black depths the Faun had found a soul, and was struggling with it toward the light of heaven"; and in Hawthorne's story of "Egotism, or the Bosom Serpent," Roderick Elliston, haunted by the belief that a serpent is lodged in his bosom, was cured of his hallucination the moment that his gentle wife whispered in, his ear the words, "Forget yourself in the idea of another." Then did he perceive that the serpent in his bosom was his own selfishness.* In "The Marble Faun" Hawthorne has given us, in the character of Donatello, an idea like that which Dr. Holmes has embodied in "Elsie Venner," namely, of a human being inheriting certain characteristics of an animal.

Almost all of Dr. Holmes' books are written to combat some theological dogma. The moral intended to be conveyed by "Elsie Venner" is that men are not responsible for many of their crimes, shortcomings, and moral and mental twists, the tendency to

* See *The Californian* magazine for August, 1881, where the writer has discussed Hawthorne's treatment of sin.

these things having been inherited. This is a favorite thesis with Dr. Holmes. He believes in free will, but thinks, with many other eminent writers, that its freedom is very much limited. The old pastor in "Elsie Venner" is led by the story of the heroine's life to adopt charitable conclusions about the total depravity of people; and Helen Darley thinks that "if, while the will lies sealed in its fountain, it may be poisoned at its very source, so that it shall flow dark and deadly through its whole course, who are we that we should judge our fellow-creatures by ourselves?" It should be remembered that Dr. Holmes does not assert his absolute belief in the possibility of animal characteristics being introduced into the nature by fœtal transmission, as in the case of Elsie Venner, but he says that he has received startling confirmation of its possibility.

The scene of "Elsie Venner" is laid in the Connecticut Valley, apparently in or near Northampton, where, in a quaint and roomy old mansion, lives Dudley Venner, the father of the heroine. To this neighborhood comes one day, as a teacher, a young man of the

"Brahmin caste," — the cultured bookish class, — named Bernard Langdon, and with him Elsie eventually falls in love. Silas Peckham, proprietor of the Apollinean Institute, employs, besides Langdon, a Miss Helen Darley, — a frail, sensitive, conscientious, overworked young teacher. Silas Peckham is admirably drawn, — only a little too hideous for the reality, — a Yankee Squeers, a hard, grasping, merciless man, "thin as if he had been split and dried ; with an ashen kind of complexion, like the tint of the food he is made of (split codfish) ; and about as sharp, tough, juiceless, and biting to deal with as the other is to the taste."   And Elsie, — "She was a splendid scowling beauty, black-browed, with a flash of white teeth which was always like a surprise when her lips parted. She wore a checkered dress, of a curious pattern, and a camel's-hair scarf twisted a little fantastically about her. . . . Black piercing eyes, not large, — a low forehead, as low as that of Clytie in the Townley bust, — black hair twisted in heavy braids, — a face that one could not help looking at for its beauty, yet that one wanted to look away from for something in its expression, and could not for those diamond eyes." She wore a barred skirt, had on her arm as a bracelet a golden asp with emerald eyes, and around her neck sometimes a torque chain, and sometimes a necklace of enamelled scales; she loved to haunt the dreaded rattlesnake cavern, especially in hot mid-summer, when the fierce poisons of nature were generated in the heats, and when her own nature became most ungovernable and serpentoid; she had castanets which she loved to rattle as an accompaniment to her dance; she had the habit of narrowing her eyes like a sleepy cat, and of drawing down, or flattening, her forehead; she had a just perceptible lisp; her hands were cold, and her glistening eyes had the power of fascinating people and making them shudder and shiver; the hysterical schoolmistress, Helen Darley, was absolutely made ill by the sight of her; her handwriting was sharp-pointed, long and slender, and she wrote on wavy, ribbed paper; for the olive-purple leaves of the white ash she had a strong and unconquerable aversion, which is said to be the case also with the rattle-snake.

A passage in the second volume of the story throws light on the mystery of this poor girl. When Helen Darley, Elsie's teacher, learns from old Sophy the secret of the "ante-natal impression which had mingled an alien element in her nature," she then understood the fascination of her cold, glittering eyes. "She knew the significance of the strange repulsion which she felt in her own intimate consciousness underlying the inexplicable attraction which drew her towards the young girl in spite of this repugnance. She began to look with new feelings on the contradictions in her moral nature, — the longing for sympathy, as shown by her wishing for Helen's company, and the impossibility of passing between the cold circle of isolation within which she had her being. The fearful truth of that instinctive feeling of hers, that there was something not human looking out of Elsie's eyes, came upon her with the sudden flash of penetrating conviction. There were two warring principles in that superb organization and proud soul. One made her a woman with all a woman's powers and longings. The other chilled all the currents of outlet for her emotions. It made her tearless and mute, when another woman would have wept and pleaded. And it infused into her soul something — it was cruel now to call it malice — which was still, watchful, and dangerous, — which waited its opportunity, and then shot like an arrow from its bow out of the coil of brooding premeditation."

The author of "Elsie Venner" wisely keeps his heroine mysteriously in the background of his picture, or rather keeps her in view, but does not permit her to speak much. This heightens the mystery and whets our curiosity. The deathbed scene of poor Elsie is as pathetic as that of the tutor in the story of Iris. A rich, deep, strange nature that of Elsie, and one that gets hold of our sympathies in a very strong manner. Who, indeed, can ever forget her? No character in English literature more eldritch and fantastical; and in English poetry but two characters at all resembling her. In Coleridge's "Christabel" the lovely Lady Geraldine exercises over the fair Christabel a fascination like that of a serpent : —

" A snake's small eye blinks dull and shy,
  And the lady's eyes they shrunk in her head,
  Each shrunk up to a serpent's eye,
  And with somewhat of malice, and more of
    dread,
  At Christabel she looked askance ! "

The Lamiæ of antiquity were fabulous monsters with the head and breast of a woman and the body of a serpent. They allured people to destruction by a soothing, strange kind of hissing. Keats gives a picture of one of these creatures : —

      " A palpitating snake,
Bright, and cirque-couchant in a dusky brake.

   .   .   .   .   .

Upon her crest she wore a wannish fire,
Sprinkled with stars, like Ariadne's tiar ;
Her head was serpent, but ah, bitter sweet !
She had a woman's mouth, with all its pearls complete."

The minor characters in " Elsie Venner " — Old Sophy, Dick Venner, Helen Darley, and the Doctor, — are finely individualized. The Sprowles' party affords the Autocrat an opportunity to display a good deal of his characteristic satirical wit, slang, and buffoonery. There is considerable fun and much local coloring in this bit of *opéra comique*, or variety show — the Sprowles' party; but the sketch is overdone, and has a touch of coarseness, unkindliness, and cockneyism in it. However, the ludicrousness of the situation grows irresistible, and, when one reaches the incident of the Deacon and the ice-cream, laughter becomes uncontrollable and violent. The Deacon mistook the ice-cream for custard, and after swallowing an immense spoonful set up a sound something between a howl and an oath ; his features assumed an expression of intense pain, his eyes staring wildly ; and, clapping his hands to his face, he rocked his head backward and forward in speechless agony. After a good deal of slapping on the back he recovers. Here is another bit of realism : " The elder Miss Spinney, to whom she made this remark, assented to it, at the same time ogling a piece of frosted cake, which she presently appropriated with great refinement of manner, — taking it between her thumb and forefinger, keeping the others well spread, and the little finger in extreme divergence, with a graceful undulation of the neck and a queer little sound in her throat, as of an *m* that wanted to get out and perished in the attempt."

The tea-party of the widow, Marilla Rowens, forms an agreeable companion-piece to the vulgarities of this party of the Sprowles. As a pendant to this theme one may add the following ludicrous advice of the " Professor ": " A few rules are worth remembering by all who attend anniversary dinners in Faneuil Hall or elsewhere. Thus : Lobsters' claws are always acceptable to children of all ages. Oranges and apples are to be taken *one at a time*, until the coat-pockets begin to become inconveniently heavy. Cakes are injured by sitting upon them ; it is, therefore, well to carry a stout tin-box of a size to hold as many pieces as there are children in the domestic circle."

" Elsie Venner " is a novel strongly flavored with rural and dialect language, of which, however, Dr. Holmes does not appear to have made quite so artistic a study as has Lowell. Some of the rural characters of the work well illustrate negatively Dr. Holmes' saying that the best specimens of New England character are raised under glass. Such Yankeeisms as the dispute, in "Elsie Venner," over the skin and shoes of the dead horse, and the negotiations of Silas Peckham for the remainder delicacies of the Sprowles' party to feed his Institute pupils with, are capital satirical strokes.

For the sake of convenience we may here consider Dr. Holmes' second novel, "The Guardian Angel," although it was not published in book-form until 1867. Perhaps the germ, or suggestion, of the work is found in this sentence from "Elsie Venner": "Every young girl ought to walk, locked close, arm in arm, between two guardian angels." Myrtle Hazard, however, has but one, the old bachelor and book-worm, Byles Gridley, whom it seems slightly absurd, by the way, to dub with the title of angel. The central idea of the story is this : There is evidence which seems to show that persons who have long been dead "may enjoy a kind of secondary and imperfect, yet self-conscious life" in our bodily tenements. "This body," says the author, " in which we journey across the isthmus between the oceans is not a private carriage, but an omnibus."   The plan of the novel is to show how in the life of Myrtle Hazard (the heroine of the book) the traits and experiences of ancestors reappear, and produce. in her strange and unaccountable actions, until love and self-sacrifice break the spell.   One of her ancestors had been accused of sorcery, or witchcraft : consequently Myrtle is full of wild and eldritch freaks and fits of waywardness.   A tinge of tropical fierceness is added to her character from the circumstance that she was born in India ; when she was a little girl she wore a scarlet dress, and was styled by a young man in the town " the fire-hang-bird," or oriole.   Another of her ancestors was burned at the stake : accordingly she is represented as being cured of her inherited taint, partly, indeed, through her love of Clement Lindsay, but chiefly through her self-denying offices of mercy in the hospitals, as well as in her self-sacrifice in the choice of a poor but noble husband : " What change was this which Myrtle had undergone since love had touched her heart, and her visions of worldly enjoyment had faded before the thought of sharing and ennobling the life of one who was worthy of her best affections, — of living for another, and finding her own noblest self in that divine office of woman? . . . If it could be that, after so many generations, the blood of her who had died for her faith could show in her descendant's veins, and the soul of that elect lady of her race look out from her far-removed offspring's dark eyes, such a transfiguration of the martyr's life and spiritual being might well seem to manifest itself in Myrtle Hazard." . . . " In the offices of mercy which she performed for sick and the wounded and the dying the dross of her nature seemed to be burned away. The conflict of mingled lives in her blood had ceased."

The plot of the work has some dramatic crises and developments, — as, for example, the scene at the rapids, the management of the will, and the finding of the old leather mitten, with the fist full of silver dollars, and the thumb of gold half-eagles. The villain, Murray Bradshaw, is almost too cold and passionless an abstraction to be lifelike; but not so Byles Gridley, author of " Thoughts on the Universe," the dear, honest, hearty old bachelor, who countermines so handsomely the plots of Bradshaw. The oily and nauseous cant of the Rev. Mr. Stoker seems as accurately reported as it could be, and the hits at the preachers are good and well-deserved. When the Rev. Mr. Stoker begins to take a *too* tender interest in the rich young beauty, Myrtle Hazard, Mrs. Hopkins advises the procuring of a bull-dog who would take the seat out of his black pantaloons the next time he called.   Old Dr. Hurlbut adds his contribution to the good cause by remarking that he always had to lay in an extra stock of valerian and assafœtida whenever there was a young minister around, — "for there's plenty of religious ravin', says he, that's nothin' but hysterics."   The vain and silly poetaster is hit off so well in Gifted Hopkins that the character at once recalls the numerous acquaintances of that genus which we have all had : the interview with the publisher is full of the richest humor.   Silence Withers and Miss Cynthia Badlam seem to have been photographed from the life. A writer in the *Spectator* thinks that the character of

Myrtle Hazard is effectually analyzed, but not reconstructed again in a unity of personality; also thinks that "to precipitate an old book-student, however keen at reading general character, into the task of unravelling and countermining the conventional conspiracy of a legal rogue like Murray Bradshaw was not a very artistic idea."

A writer in *The Nation* for November 14, 1867, offered the following caustic criticism on "The Guardian Angel" : —

"What 'goes without saying,' as the French put it, Dr. Holmes is very apt to say; that, we believe, is the thing which chiefly interferes with our enjoyment of his works." The reviewer cites as instances the talk of Professor Gridley, and the hit at the Calvinists in the dismal ululations of the hell-fire hymns of those low-spirited Christian pessimists, Cousin Silence and Miss Cynthia. "Dr. Holmes," he continues, "goes through his story, — too often bearing on hard when only the lightest touch would have been pleasing, not to say sufferable; sternly breaking on his wheel the deadest of bugs and butterflies." —"There is a good deal of triteness and dulness and flippancy in his book." — "When he had written 'The Autocrat of the Breakfast-Table,' Dr. Holmes would have done well, as it has since appeared, had he ceased from satire. That series of papers gave him a brilliant reputation, which from that time forward he has gone on damaging, diminishing it by each new book; diminishing the brilliance of it, at any rate, though it may well enough be that he has extended it among more people. He has never stopped hammering on the same nail which he hit on the head when he first struck. 'The Professor' took away something from the estimation in which we had been holding the 'Autocrat'; 'Elsie Venner' took away a little more; and 'The Guardian Angel' takes away a larger portion than was removed by either of the others.

"We speak of the author as a satirist. That he is, mainly; he is hardly to be called a novelist. His characters are figures labelled and set up to be fired at, or are names about which a love-story is told, or they embody some physiologico-psychological theory; but they are never to be called characters in any true sense of the word."

The year 1861 saw the opening of the Civil War waged for the preservation of the Union and of the rights of man. There is nothing like the glowing furnace of a great moral conflict to purge away the dross and slag from men's natures. Dr. Holmes possesses, or possessed, a generous share of those very human frailties of character which do so much to level distinctions among men. He has probably written and spoken more offensive ineptitudes about "the quality," the "swell-fronts," the "Brahmin caste," "the unpaved districts," etc., than any other writer in America. The fierce war struggle, and the close sympathy it excited between all classes, served to take a good deal of this pride out of him. He says somewhere, " The camp is deprovincializing us very fast. . . . It takes all the nonsense out of everybody, or ought to do so, to see how fairly the real manhood of a country is distributed over its surface."

Professor Holmes' attitude on the slavery question in the ante-bellum days is not wholly such as we could wish it had been. Like so many others in the early days of abolitionism, he thought that offensive measures against the South would result disastrously to the integrity of the Union. He therefore took to the fence, unwilling to identify himself fully with either party in the dispute. In an address before the New England Society of New York City he expressed admiration for the manly logic of the faction of the extreme left, — the Abolitionists, the "melanophiles." He said : "We have respect for the men of the extreme party; namely, the respect which we feel for Othello in his murderous delusion. But then we also demand consistency in the party of the centre and the moderate left: they should either annul the Constitution, or else keep it in its evident spirit; not act double, crying out against slavery, and yet clinging to the Constitution."

A citation from a very careful and scholarly writer who was an active participant in the stormy struggles of the war will throw more light on this topic than we can get from any other source: "Boston," says Mr. F. B. Sanborn,* "then abounded with those natural Tories, who, in the rough dialect of

* In his excellent and valuable article in "The Homes and Haunts of our Elder Poets."

their radical opposites, were styled 'Hunkers.' They made up the powerful class which controlled the market, the college, and the drawing-room ; they opened or closed at will the avenues of preferment for young men of talent ; they ignored Emerson, loathed Garrison, detested Parker, ridiculed Alcott and Margaret Fuller, tolerated Sumner and Phillips for a time on account of their talents, and then quietly sent them to Coventry.   In this well-fed, well-bred minority, supported by a well-fed, but ill-bred majority, Dr. Holmes was content to remain for years, scoffing at reformers now and then to please his audience, but chafing a little under the dull oppression of the popular theology, against which he finally revolted as completely as Theodore Parker had done before him.   In his 'Urania,' written in 1846, Dr. Holmes went so far as to denounce John Quincy Adams, by implication, as an enemy of the Union, while that 'old man eloquent' was fighting the battle of freedom in Congress.   The poet exclaimed :—

' Chiefs of New England ! by your sires' renown,
  Dash the red torches of the rebel down !
  Flood his black hearthstone till its flames expire,
  Though your old Sachem fanned his council fire.'

"This 'old Sachem' was Adams, and the 'rebel' was the Abolitionist, not the slave-holder, who turned out in fact to be so. Patriotism, always strong in Dr. Holmes, united with Toryism to hold him on the 'Hunker' side until toward the beginning of the Civil War, or, perhaps, no later than 1857, when the anti-slavery party definitely gained control of Massachusetts, re-electing Sumner to the Senate almost unanimously. Indeed, in 1856, when Sumner was assaulted by the South Carolina bully, Dr. Holmes at a public dinner in Boston denounced the outrage as an assault upon the Union. And when the Civil War broke out none stood more firmly by the cause of the North than the laughing Professor. He sent his eldest son to the fight, and saw him twice or thrice wounded, without shrinking from the sacrifice which his country demanded. This manly attitude, from which Dr. Holmes never receded, atoned, in the eyes even of his cousin Wendell Phillips, for the early antagonism to what few men then recognized as the sacred cause of civilization."

Mr. Sanborn may well say that the war

record of Holmes atoned for his early indifference. We hardly expect poets to be lovers of strife, and it is not much wonder that Holmes took the attitude he did toward abolitionism. But read his patriotic war poems, his splendid Fourth of July Oration, delivered in Boston in 1863, and his many patriotic articles in the *Atlantic Monthly*, if you would know how glowing and earnest was his love of the Union and of human rights. His inherited toryism and conservatism made it harder for him than for others to grieve at the subjugation of an inferior class: as late as 1882 he was taken to task by a Boston paper for depreciation of the Irish in their efforts to free their throats from the teeth of the British bull-dog. But of his patriotism no one can doubt. His Fourth of July Oration was delivered at one of the gloomiest moments of the war, when Lee was in the heart of Pennsylvania, and just before the capture of Vicksburg. The argument of the oration is this : The principle of self-government involves the right of free discussion and free political action. The exercise of this right led to the war between slavery and freedom, and in striving to preserve the Union the North vindicates a principle fatal to the existence of slavery. Hear a few sentences : —

" By those wounds of living heroes, by those graves of fallen martyrs, by the corpses of your children, and the claims of your children's children yet unborn, in the name of outraged honor, in the interest of violated sovereignty, for the life of an imperilled nation, for the sake of men everywhere, and of our common humanity, for the glory of God, and the advancement of his kingdom on earth, your country calls upon you to stand by her through good report and through evil report, in triumph and in defeat."

In the *Atlantic Monthly* for October, 1861, Dr. Holmes published an article entitled " The Wormwood Cordial of History." It is an historical paper, designed to give comfort to the people of the North after their defeat at the battle of Bull Run. The Romans were beaten at Lake Trasimenus and at Cannae, and the Prussians were beaten at Jena ; yet both peoples retrieved those disasters, and so will the North. The fable of " The Front

Teeth and the Grinders " will bear repeating : —

" Once on a time a mutiny arose among the teeth of a man, in good health, and blessed with a sound constitution, commonly known as Uncle Samuel. The cutting teeth, or *incisors*, and the eye-teeth, or *canines*, though not nearly so many, all counted, nor so large nor so strong as the grinders, and by no means so white, but, on the contrary, very much discolored, began to find fault with the grinders as not good enough company for them. The eye-teeth being very sharp, and fitted for seizing and tearing, and standing out taller than the rest, claimed to lead them. Presently one of them complained that it ached very badly, and then another and another. Very soon the cutting teeth, which pretended they were supplied by the same nerve, and were proud of it, began to ache also. They all agreed that it was the fault of the grinders.

" About this time, Uncle Samuel, having used his old tooth-brush (which was never a good one, having no stiffness in the bristles) for four years, took a new one, recommended to him by a great number of people as a homely but useful article. Thereupon all the front teeth, one after another, declared that Uncle Samuel meant to scour them white, which was a thing they would never submit to, though the whole civilized world was calling on them to do so. So they all insisted on getting out of the sockets in which they had grown and stood for so many years. But the wisdom teeth spoke up for the others, and said :—

" ' Nay, there be but twelve of you front-teeth, and there be twenty of us grinders. We are the strongest, and a good deal nearest the muscles and the joint, but we cannot spare you. We have put up with your black stains, your jumping aches, and your snappish looks, and now we are not going to let you go, under the pretence that you are going to be scrubbed white if you stay. You don't work half so hard as we do, but you can bite the food well enough, which we can grind so much better than you. We belong to each other. You must stay.'

" Thereupon the front-teeth, first the ca-nines, or dog-teeth, next the incisors, or cutting-teeth, proceeded to aeclare themselves out of their sockets, and no longer belonging to the jaws of 'Uncle Samuel.'

"Then Uncle Samuel arose in his wrath, and shut his jaws tightly together, and swore that he would keep them shut till those aching and discolored teeth of his went to pieces in their sockets, if need were, rather than have them drawn, standing, as some of them did, at the very opening of his throat and stomach.

"And now, if you will please to observe, all those teeth are beginning to ache worse than ever, and to decay very fast, so that it will take a great deal of gold to stop the holes that are forming in them. But the great white grinders are as sound as ever, and will remain so until Uncle Samuel thinks the time has come for opening his mouth. In the mean time they keep on grinding in a quiet way, though the others have had to stop biting for a long time. When Uncle Samuel opens his mouth they will be as ready for work as ever; but those poor discolored teeth will be tender for a great while, and never be so strong as they were before they foolishly declared themselves out of their sockets."

"Soundings from the Atlantic" is the title of a volume made up chiefly of papers first published in the *Atlantic Monthly*. They are very readable, — breezy and light as well as solid. Those on the photograph and the stereoscope are certainly unique in their combination of airy humorous treatment with solid scientific discussion, or teaching. He has made the subject of the photograph and the stereoscope in their æsthetic relations peculiarly his own by the thoroughness and enthusiasm of his investigations and experiments. On one page he gives you a charmingly poetical and lucid description of the way a photograph is made, and of his amateur apprenticeship to the art; and on the next page you have a record of original scientific observations and studies. It is probably known to but few that to Dr. Holmes' inventive genius we owe the stereoscope in the convenient form in which it is now made; the public obtained his improvements unpatented, and consequently at a lower price. There is room for but a single paragraph from the article on the stereoscope and the stereograph : —

"We were just now stereographed ourselves, at a moment's warning, as if we were fugitives from justice. A skeleton shape, of about a man's height, its head covered with a black veil, glided across the floor, faced us, lifted its veil, and took a preliminary look. When we had grown sufficiently rigid in our attitude of studied ease, and got our umbrella into a position of thoughtful carelessness, and put our features with much effort into an unconstrained aspect of cheerfulness tempered with dignity, of manly firmness blended with womanly sensibility, of courtesy, as much as to imply, 'You know me, sir,' toned or sized, as one may say, with something of the self-assertion of a human soul which reflects proudly, 'I am superior to all this,'—when, I say, we were all right, the spectral Mokanna dropped his long veil, and his waiting slave put a sensitive tablet under its folds."

From an article on "Sun-Painting and Sun-Sculpture" the following is extracted : —

"We may regard those shadows of bodies which are fixed by photography as films, or subtle effluences, thrown off from the bodies themselves.   Hence, we may say that "we lift an impalpable scale from the surface of the Pyramids.   We slip off from the dome of St. Peter's that other imponderable dome which fitted it so closely that it betrays every scratch on the original.   We skim off a thin, dry cuticle from the rapids of Niagara, and lay it on our unmoistened paper without breaking a bubble or losing a speck of foam.   We steal a landscape from its lawful owners, and defy the charge of dishonesty.   We skin the flints by the wayside, and nobody accuses us of meanness."

An amusing chapter in "Soundings" is the "Visit to the Asylum for Aged and Decayed Punsters."   Here are some of the puns of the afflicted inmates :—

"'Don't you see Webster *ers* in the words cent*er* and theat*er?*

"'If he spells leather *lether*, and feather *fether*, isn't there danger that he'll give us a *bad spell of weather?*

"'Look!' said the Director, — 'that is our Centenarian.'

"The ancient man crawled towards us,

cocked one eye, with which he seemed to see a little, up at us, and said, —

" ' Sarvant, young gentleman. Why is a — a — a — like a — a — a — ? Give it up ? Because it's a — a — a — a — .'

" He smiled a pleasant smile, as if it were all plain enough.

" ' One hundred and seven last Christmas,' said the Director."

As the Autocrat assures us that a pun does not commonly justify a blow in return, we are encouraged to quote here two or three good ones from his own poems, as this : —

" Long metre answers for a common song,
    Though common metre does not answer long."

Or this : —

" Thus great Achilles, who had shown his zeal
    In healing wounds, died of a wounded heel."

Or this first stanza from the poem read at the meeting of the Harvard Alumni in 1857 : —

" I thank you, Mr. President, you've kindly broke
        the ice ;
Virtue should always be the first, — I'm only
        SECOND VICE —

(A vice is something with a screw that's made to
   hold its jaw
Till some old file has played away upon an ancient
   saw.) "

There are two more interesting papers in
" Soundings from the Atlantic."   " The Human Wheel, its Spokes and Felloes," is an
interesting illustrated paper about human
locomotion with special reference to the
wooden leg invented by B. F. Palmer, and to
the shoe-lasts of Dr. J. C. Plumer.   Palmer's
wooden leg seems to be as great a wonder in
its way as that wonderful golden limb of Miss
Kilmansegg.   The following sentences of Dr.
Holmes explain the title of his article : " Man,"
he says, " is a wheel with two spokes, his legs,
and two fragments of a tire, his feet.   He
rolls successively on each of these fragments
from the heel to the toe.   If he had spokes
enough, he would go round and round as the
boys do when they 'make a wheel' with
their four limbs for its spokes."

" The Great Instrument " is a paper de-
scribing Walcker's organ in Music Hall, Boston.   The organ is a choir of nearly six

thousand vocal throats, four key-boards, two pedals, and twelve pairs of bellows. The façade was designed by the Herter Brothers and Hammatt Billings.

Two or three articles put forth in 1864 call for notice. "The Minister Plenipotentiary" is an eulogium of Henry Ward Beecher for his valuable services to the Union in Great Britain. Dr. Holmes calls his visit "a more remarkable embassy than that of any envoy who has represented us in Europe since Franklin pleaded the cause of the young Republic at the Court of Versailles." The essayist gives a lively and complete account of Mr. Beecher's impassioned speeches in the great centres of Britain, and tells how the populace covered the walls in London with blood-red, threatening placards and hired their "Chokers," their "Hustlers," and their burglars to waylay him.

"Our Progressive Independence" is a long and thoughtful paper on the relation of Great Britain to our own country, and was suggested by the blind and selfish policy of the mother-country in respect of our Civil War. Alluding to the stimulus to invention which constitutional freedom from Great Britain necessarily produced among us, the essayist says that the Yankee whittling a shingle with his jack-knife has been regarded as a caricature, but that it is in fact an unconscious symbolization of the plastic or inventive instinct which rises by gradations from the shingle to the clothes-pin, the apple-parer, the mowing-machine, the wooden truss-bridge, the clipper-ship, the carved figure-head, the Cleopatra of the World's Exhibition.

One invention especially, the discovery of anæsthesia, or the administering of ether for the alleviation of pain, goes far in itself alone toward paying back the debt we owe to the Old World. One evening in October, 1846, says the Doctor, a professional brother called upon him; shutting the door carefully, he looked nervously around, and then told of the wonderful discovery in the operating-room whereby a patient could be made pleasantly and safely insensible to pain for a limited period. He produced a communication which he had just written out for a learned society in Boston, the first ever drawn up on the subject. "In one fortnight's time," he said, "all Europe will be ablaze with this discovery"; and so it proved; in a few weeks every surgeon in the world knew the miraculous process. So much for one discovery, and one step in our progressive independence.

As for our early political literature, it is no wonder that the British did not understand its power and beauty. They did not understand their own constitution until De Lolme, a Swiss exile, explained it to them. " One British tourist after another visited this country, with his eye-glass at his eye, and his small vocabulary of 'Very odd!' for all that was new to him; his 'Quite so!' for whatever was noblest in thought and deed; his 'Very clever!' for the encouragement of genius; and his 'All that sort of thing, you know!' for the less marketable virtues and heroisms not to be found in the Cockney price-current. They came, they saw, they made their books, but no man got from them any correct idea of what the Great Republic meant in the history of civilization. For this the British people had to wait until De Tocqueville, a Frenchman, made it in some degree palpable to English comprehension." The odious sneers of Dr. Samuel Johnson, in his "Taxation no Tyranny," Holmes whimsically calls "The coprolites of a literary megatherium." Johnson was succeeded by Carlyle — a man whom his elephantine predecessor in London would have hated for his nationality, and knocked down with his dictionary for his assaults on the English language. Dr. Holmes thinks Prescott did more than any other to establish the independence of American literature. He was the first who worked with an adequate literary apparatus, and at the same time cast his costly and learned researches in a pictorial and popular form. It was not however from England, but from the Continent of Europe, that the recognition of his genius first came. The essay closes with a reference to the fact that the attitude of England toward us in the Civil War, the dense ignorance of us and our affairs that it betrayed, and the blind contempt which always accompanies ignorance, served completely to destroy in the minds of our people that implicit and unquestioning deference to English standards and models which had so long characterized us as a nation.

Professor Holmes was one of the illustrious company that followed the remains of the author of "The Scarlet Letter" to their final resting-place in Sleepy Hollow. With the closing paragraph of the unfinished "Dolliver Romance," says Dr. Holmes, "the mystic music of the poet's voice is suddenly hushed, and we seem to hear instead the tolling of a bell in the far distance. The procession of shadowy characters which was gathering in our imaginations about the ancient man and the little child who come so clearly before our sight seems to fade away, and in its place a slow-pacing train winds through the village-road and up the wooded hillside until it stops at a little opening among the tall trees. There the bed is made in which he whose dreams had peopled our common life with shapes and thoughts of beauty and wonder is to take his rest. . . .

"The day of his burial was the bridal day of the season, perfect in light as if heaven were looking on, perfect in air as if Nature herself were sighing for our loss. The orchards were all in fresh flower,

' One boundless blush, one white-empurpled shower
  Of mingled blossoms ' ;

the banks were literally blue with violets ; the elms were putting out their tender leaves, just in that passing aspect which Raphael loved to pencil in the backgrounds of his holy pictures, not as yet printing deep shadows, but only mottling the sunshine at their feet. The birds were in full song ; the pines were musical with the soft winds they sweetened. All was in faultless accord, and every heart was filled with the beauty that flooded the landscape."

CHAPTER VII.

BEACON STREET.

Down the hill crowned by the State House, Beacon Street stretches straight away westward for a mile or more. For the first half of that distance it skirts the Common and the beautiful, flower-filled Public Garden, and has at its side a great elm-arched tunnel of leaves, — the Beacon Street mall, most delightful of walks. It is a fine sight to stand at night at the head of the street and see the long fairy-like perspective of golden lamp-globes winking and gleaming as if to rival the stars above them. On pleasant afternoons, too, you will see the wealth and blood (equine and human) of the city on this street. The people in the carriages are mostly free from the melancholy, corpse-like appearance of their Fifth Avenue brethren; and the equestrians and the pedestrians — where will you see ruddier and manlier physiques, or happier, healthier children? Yet to one coming suddenly into Beacon Street from thoughtful Cambridge, from the aristocracy of mind to the aristocracy of wealth, a slight lowering of the intellectual temperature is perceptible. As for the people, they are either a community of happy drones in the national hive, or they are engaged in severe mental toil for the benefit of the republic. Which is it? But however it may be with others, the reproach of idleness cannot be visited upon one inhabitant, at least, of this street; for in the brick house numbered 296, situated on that extension of Beacon Street which formerly went by the name of the Mill Dam, lives the laureate of Boston, the white-haired poet of a hundred civic banquets, prolific author, honored ex-professor, the sunniest-hearted man in the city, and one of the most popular. Professor Holmes removed from 164 Charles Street to his Beacon Street residence in 1871. There is a tiny grass-plot in front of the house, and in small letters over the door-bell is the familiar name. Entering by a spacious hall, the visitor, if on terms of intimacy, is ushered into the study in the rear of the house. The room is light and cheerful, its bay-window giving directly upon the River Charles, with Memorial Tower in Cambridge looming up in the distance ; — the old view, you see, and one which the poet has enjoyed now for twenty-three years. Let him describe one phase of it as seen from the Beacon Street study : —

"Through my north window, in the wintry
    weather, —
  My airy oriel on the river shore, —
I watch the sea-fowl as they flock together
    Where late the boatman flashed his dripping
    oar.

"The gull, high floating, like a sloop unladen,
    Lets the loose water waft him as it will;
The duck, round-breasted as a rustic maiden,
    Paddles and plunges, busy, busy still.

"I see the solemn gulls in council sitting
  On some broad ice-floe, pondering long and
    late,
While overhead the home-bound ducks are flit-
    ting,
  And leave the tardy conclave in debate,

" Those weighty questions in their breasts revolv-
       ing
  Whose deeper meaning science never learns,
Till at some reverend elder's look dissolving,
  The speechless senate silently adjourns."

Besides the bay-window the study has two
circular windows which throw light upon the
alcoves between the bookcases, as well as
upon the microscopical apparatus which
stands ready for its owner's use. Three
sides of the apartment are completely lined
with books, —

" A mingled race, the wreck of chance and time,
  That talk all tongues and breathe of every clime,
  Each knows his place, and each may claim his
     part.
In some quaint corner of his master's heart."

                            The Study.

Dr. Holmes' private library is rich in rare
medical treatises and in literary treasures :
his readers will find references to these books
scattered all through his works. The writing-
desk is in the centre of the room, and over it
hangs a drop-light. There are easy chairs, and

lambrequins, and a large mirror over the fire-place, while near the door hangs the original portrait of "Dorothy Q." Another portrait in the room is by Copley, and represents the Rev. Dr. Samuel Cooper, who was a friend of Benjamin Franklin, and preached in the Brattle Street Church to some of the ancestors of Dr. Holmes. In the drawing-room just across the hall from the library are to be seen some fine reproductions of paintings of the old masters, made by a peculiar process.

" The Poet at the Breakfast-Table " (1873) was first published, like its predecessors, in periodical instalments. It is the weakest work of the Breakfast-Table Series, and much of it had better have been left un-written. The vein has been worked so long that it "pans out" — nothing, or next to nothing. We manage to work up a trifle of sympathy for the Little Gentleman, and take an interest in a few brilliant parts of the work: the poem called " Epilogue to the Breakfast-Table Series " is capital; but these are redeeming features in an intolerably dull book, in which the continual straining after effect wearies us, and the homilies and dull commonplaces of experience make us yawn, and anxiously measure, from time to time, with thumb and finger, the amount still left to be read. Dr. Holmes has written many fine and valuable papers since 1873, but certainly about that time people would have been justified in quoting against him two lines of his own :—

"'Why won't he stop writing?' Humanity cries ;
    The answer is briefly, 'He can't if he tries.'"

But the reader shall have one or two fine extracts from the " Poet at the Breakfast-Table." First, a description of the piano-player : —

" I have been to hear some music-pounding. It was a young woman, with as many white muslin flounces around her as the planet Saturn has rings, that did it. She gave the music-stool a twirl or two, and fluffed down on to it like a whirl of soapsuds in a hand-basin. Then she pushed up her cuffs as if she was going to fight for the champion's belt. Then she worked her wrists and her hands, to limber 'em, I suppose, and spread out her fingers till they looked as though they would pretty much cover the key-board, from the growling end to the little squeaking one. Then those two hands of hers made a jump at the keys as if they were a couple of tigers coming down on a flock of black and white sheep, and the piano gave a great howl as if its tail had been trod on. Dead stop, — so still you could hear your hair growing. Then another jump, and another howl, as if the piano had two tails, and you had trod on both of 'em at once, and then a grand clatter and scramble and string of jumps, up and down, back and forward, one hand over the other, like a stampede of rats and mice more than like anything I call music."

·Next, a whimsical account of a poor ghost who visits a library some years after his departure from the body, and discovers, to his indignation, the stupid blunders that have been made by his biographer : —

" *'Born in July, 1776 !'* And my honored father killed at the battle of Bunker Hill ! Atrocious libeller ! to slander one's family at the start, after such a fashion !

" *' The death of his parents left him in charge of his Aunt Nancy, whose tender care took the place of those parental attentions which should have guided and protected his infant years, and consoled him for the severity of another relative.'*

"— Aunt *Nancy!* It was Aunt *Betsey,* you fool! Aunt Nancy used to — she has been dead these eighty years, so there is no use in mincing matters — she used to keep a bottle and a stick, and when she had been tasting a drop out of the bottle the stick used to come off of the shelf, and I had to taste that. And here she is made a saint of, and poor Aunt Betsey, that did everything for me, is slandered by implication as a horrid tyrant!

"' *The subject of this commemorative history was remarkable for a precocious development of intelligence. An old nurse, who saw him at the very earliest period of his existence, is said to have spoken of him as one of the most promising infants she had seen in her long experience. At school he was equally remarkable, and at a tender age he received a paper adorned with a cut, inscribed* REWARD OF MERIT.'

— "I don't doubt the nurse said that, — there were several promising children born about that time. As for *cuts*, I got more from the schoolmaster's rattan than in any other shape. Didn't one of 'em split a Gunter's scale into three pieces over the palm of my hand? And didn't I grin when I saw the pieces fly? No humbug, now, about my boyhood!"

The only wonder is that the penning of the foregoing lines did not bring down at once upon the Autocrat an army of biographers, with assurances of sympathy, and with the offer of immediate justice in the shape of a hot-pressed, gilt-edged biography, to be written in the warm present, when there is little chance of error respecting Aunt Nancy and Aunt Betsey.

In an appreciative review of "Exotics," a little book of delicate poetical translations, by James Freeman Clarke, and his daughter, Miss L. Clarke, Dr. Holmes has embodied (in the *Atlantic* for September, 1875) a description of the poet's state of mind and body when writing, which will be recognized by all who have indulged in poetical creation as true in all its details. It is impossible to condense or rewrite this bit of analysis. He

says that, when composing, the poet is a
medium, a clairvoyant. "The will is first
called in requisition to exclude interfering
outward impressions and alien trains of
thought. After a certain time the second
state or adjustment of the poet's double consciousness (for he has two states, just as the
somnambulists have) sets up its own auto-
matic movement, with its special trains of
ideas and feelings in the thinking and emotional centres. As soon as the fine frenzy,
or *quasi* trance-state, is fairly established, the
consciousness watches the torrent of thoughts
and arrests the ones wanted, singly with their
fitting expression, or in groups of fortunate
sequences which he cannot better by after
treatment. As the poetical vocabulary is
limited, and its plasticity lends itself only to
certain moulds, the mind works under great
difficulty, at least until it has acquired by
practice such handling of language that every
possibility of rhythm or rhyme offers itself
actually or potentially to the clairvoyant perception simultaneously with the thought it is
to embody. Thus poetical composition is the
most intense, the most exciting, and there-

fore the most exhausting of mental exercises. It is exciting because its mental states are a series of revelations and surprises; intense on account of the double strain upon the attention. The poet is not the same man who seated himself an hour ago at his desk, with the dust-cart and the gutter, or the duck-pond and the hay-stack and the barnyard fowls beneath his window. He is in the forest with the song-birds; he is on the mountain-top with the eagles. He sat down in rusty broadcloth, he is arrayed in the imperial purple of his singing robes. Let him alone now if you are wise, for you might as well have pushed the arm that was finishing the smile of a Madonna, or laid a rail before a train that had a queen on board, as thrust your untimely question on this half cataleptic child of the muse, who hardly knows whether he is in the body or out of the body. And do not wonder if, when the fit is over, he is in some respects like one who is recovering after an excess of the baser stimulants. . . . 'Song intoxicates the poet.' His brain rings with it for hours or days or weeks after it has chimed itself through his consciousness. The vibration

dies away gradually like the tremor of a bell
which has been struck, and the medium comes
to himself again.   What a pity that the passion and the fever and the delirium are not a
measure of the excellence of the product of
the poetic trance!"

A valuable and unique article by Dr. Holmes
on the "Physiology of Versification and the
Harmonies of Organic and Animal Life"
should be rescued from the pages of the *Boston Medical and Surgical Journal* (January 7,
1875).   Following is an abstract of it : The
secret of our success or failure as social beings depends far more largely on our bodily
health than our friends suppose.

The rhythmical movements of the respiration and the pulse are the time-keepers of the
body, with a constant ratio of one inspiration
to every four beats of the heart.

Respiration has an intimate relation to the
structure of metrical compositions.   The reason why octosyllabic verse is so easy to read
aloud is that it follows more exactly than any
other measure the natural rhythm of the respiration.   In reading, for example, such eight-
syllable verse as that of "In Memoriam," or

"The Lay of the Last Minstrel," it is found that about twenty lines can be uttered in a minute ; now the average number of expirations a minute is also twenty, showing that one line is read for each expiration, with an inspiration at the end of the line. The peculiar majesty of the ten-syllable, or heroic line, comes from the fact that its pronunciation requires a longer respiration than ordinary ; hence a sense of effort and slowness. The cæsura comes in at irregular intervals, to be sure, and serves as a breathing-place, but its management requires care in reading, and entirely breaks up the natural rhythm of breathing. The fourteen-syllable line of Chapman's Homer and of our hymn-books ("common metre") is exceedingly easy reading, because broken up into short, alternate lines of six and eight syllables. The twelve-syllable line — that of Drayton's Polyolbion — is the most irksome of all, owing to its unphysiological construction. The fourteen-syllable line we easily divide in half in reading, but the twelve-syllable one is too much for one expiration and not enough for two, and for this reason has been instinctively avoided by nearly all poets. Parts of Tennyson's "Maud" are written in fourteen and seventeen-syllable verse, and are very difficult to read aloud.

But then there is the personal equation to be taken into the account. A person of ample chest and quiet temperament may breathe habitually only fourteen times in a minute, and to him the heroic measure will be very easy reading; whereas a narrow-chested, nervous person, breathing oftener than twenty times a minute, may find such seven-syllable verse as that of Dyer's "Grongar Hill" more agreeable to his respiration than the heroic line; and a quick-breathing child will recite with pleasure Mother Goose melodies when long metres would make it catch its breath. Perhaps there may be other organic rhythms; perhaps *accent* is suggested by or connected with the movements of the pulse; it is a fact that twenty acts of respiration correspond to eighty arterial pulsations, and that twenty eight-syllable lines, corresponding to these eighty pulsations, have exactly eighty accents. Finally, there is the well-known coincidence between the average pulsations of the arteries and the number of steps taken in a minute; as we increase the rapidity of our steps, the heart increases the rapidity of its beats.

In 1879 the publishers of the *Atlantic Monthly*, with which Dr. Holmes had been associated as a contributor ever since its establishment, twenty-two years previously, resolved to give a breakfast in honor of the Autocrat's seventieth birthday, and the third day of December was chosen as a more convenient time than August the twenty-ninth for the celebration of the event. The breakfast was given at the Hotel Brunswick, in the richly and massively furnished parlors of which the reception took place, previous to the adjournment to the dining-room. Dr. Holmes and his daughter, Mrs. Sargent, received the one hundred guests of the occasion, and were assisted in that ceremony by Mrs. Harriet Beecher Stowe, Ralph Waldo Emerson, John G. Whittier, and Mrs. Julia Ward Howe. The breakfast proper lasted from one-and-a-half to four o'clock in the afternoon. The six tables — four of them lengthwise, and two crosswise — were well filled (the Autocrat at the head), and the masculine black of the company was relieved by a sprinkle here and there of bright feminine colors. Mr. H. O. Houghton and Mr. W. D. Howells presided, — Mr. Houghton being seated between Dr. Holmes and Mrs. Stowe, and Mr. Howells between Mr. Emerson and Mrs. Howe. Nearly every author of eminence in America was either present in person, or sent a letter of regret and congratulation. The picture of this flowery banquet, where sat the laureate of Boston, surrounded by the most eminent authors of America, many of them the cherished friends of a lifetime, gives one a great sense of satisfaction, as one thinks of it; the idea so happy, so fitting. The generous rivalry of the tributes, the unusual excellence of the poems and the speeches, and the sunshine diffused over the whole by the genial presence of him who had for a lifetime been the light and soul of a long series of similar happy occasions, — all these things combined to make the Holmes Breakfast the crowning event of the kind in the literary history of the city. The poem read by Dr. Holmes is (perhaps with

the exception of "The Chambered Nautilus ")
the finest creation of his genius. Where in
all literature will you find a more exquisite
poetical description of old age than in "The
Iron Gate " ? Where finer imagery, melody,
pathos ? —

" Still as the silver cord gets worn and slender,
  Its lightened task-work tugs with lessening
    strain,
Hands get more helpful, voices, grown more
    tender,
  Soothe with their softened tones the slumberous
    brain."

Youth longs and manhood strives, but age re-
    members,
  Sits by the raked-up ashes of the past,
Spreads its thin hands above the whitening em-
    bers
  That warm its creeping life-blood till the last.

. . . . . .

But Nature lends her mirror of illusion
  To win from saddening scenes our age-dimmed
    eyes,
And misty day-dreams blend in sweet confusion
  The wintry landscape and the summer skies.

So when the iron portal shuts behind us,
    And life forgets us in its noise and whirl,
Visions that shunned the glaring noonday find us,
    And glimmering starlight shows the gates of
        pearl.

   .   .   .   .   .

And now with grateful smile and accents cheerful,
    And warmer heart than look or word can tell,
In simplest phrase, — these traitorous eyes are
      tearful, —
    Thanks, Brothers, Sisters, — Children, — and
      farewell ! ”

One who was present has said that the intonation of that word "farewell" will never cease to ring in the ears of those who felt the throb of feeling with which it was spoken.

The other poems read were by Whittier, Cranch, Stedman, J. T. Trowbridge, William Winter, Mrs. Julia Ward Howe, Mrs. Helen Hunt, and others. Here are three stanzas of Mr. Winter's beautiful poem : —

    “ At first we thought him but a jest,
        A ray of laughter, quick to fade ;
    We did not dream how richly blest
        In his pure life, our lives were made ;
    Till soon the aureole shone, confest,
        Upon his crest.

" When violets fade the roses blow ;
　　When laughter dies the passions wake ;
His royal song, that slept below,
　　Like Arthur's sword beneath the lake,
Long since has flashed its fiery glow
　　O'er all we know.

　　.　　　　.　　　　.　　　　.

"The silken tress, the mantling wine,
　　Red roses, summer's whispering leaves,
The lips that kiss, the hands that twine,
　　The heart that loves, the heart that grieves,
They all have found a deathless shrine
　　In his rich line ! "

Many interesting letters from those who
were unable to be present were read. Among
them was this characteristic letter from John
Holmes, the brother of the poet : —

　　　　　　" CAMBRIDGE, Nov. 14, 1879.

" GENTLEMEN, — I cannot decline your
kind invitation without a word of preface.
Between my brother and myself there has
never been but one subject of rivalry, — that
of age ; and there I long since gained the day,
— having found myself generally considered
his superior on this point.   This circumstance

has placed me in a *quasi* paternal attitude toward him, and gives me a double claim to enjoy the pleasant evidence of his success which you now offer.

"As intermediary between my brother and a casual portion of society I have been made the depositary of many favorable opinions in his behalf, and can honestly say that I have never accepted any commission for my services, in the way of personal compliment. Employed, as I so often have been, as an opaque sentient medium to transmit rays of appreciation without loss of heat by absorption, I am pleased to report to you the uniform success of the experiment.

" I wish my brother all that he would himself select from the bouquets of good-will that are made up for such occasions, and freely tender him that title to seniority of which I have so long deprived him.

"As on a former occasion, I feel unwilling to seat myself among our *littérateurs*, on the score of my scant authorship, — even with the added plea of brotherhood to your guest.

"Very truly yours,

"John Holmes."

Lowell has aptly called John Holmes "one of those choice poets who will not tarnish their bright fancies by publication." And, indeed, those of us here in Cambridge who have had frequent tastes, in social circles, of the "Lambish quintessence of John," feel pretty confident, and dare maintain it, too, that as for the rich sunshine and the pure honey of artless humor, we are not poorer than Boston; that city possesses Oliver Wendell Holmes, and Cambridge has his fraternal counterpart. He has not published much, but that little is choice.

But to return to the Autocrat. The spring of 1882 saw the death of Longfellow, Emerson, and Darwin, all of whom passed away within a few weeks of each other. That was a sad spring in Boston: there was a troubled look in people's faces, and the mute inquiry, "Who next?" To the memory of each of his brother-poets, Dr. Holmes dedicated a masterly oration. The qualities of Emerson he sums up in these words : —

"He was a man of excellent common-sense, with a genius so uncommon that he seemed like an exotic transplanted from some

angelic nursery. His character was so blame-
less, so beautiful, that it was rather a standard
to judge others by than to find a place for on
the scale of comparison. Looking at life with
the profoundest sense of its infinite significance, he was yet a cheerful optimist, almost
too hopeful, peeping into every cradle to see
if it did not hold a babe with the halo of a
new Messiah about it. He enriched the
treasure-house of literature, but what was far
more, he enlarged the boundaries of thought
for the few that followed him and the many
who never knew, and do not know to-day,
what hand it was which took down their
prison walls. He was a preacher who taught
that the religion of humanity included both
those of Palestine, nor those alone, and
taught it with such consecrated lips that the
narrowest bigot was ashamed to pray for him,
as from a footstool nearer to the throne."

The summers of our poet have been passed
.not only at Pittsfield, and at the old homestead
in Cambridge, but also, of late years, at the
home of his daughter, Mrs. Sargent, in
Beverly Farms. This is one of the most
fashionable suburban villages, or collection of

villas, near Boston. It is by the sea, and north of Boston some eighteen miles. Part of the way to Beverly, *via* the Eastern Railway, lies through wide lagoons, covered with the sea, at high tide. If it is autumn you will see around you innumerable half-drowned haycocks (the marsh-grass stacked on piles out of reach of the water), and to the right the Lynn Railroad, and Revere Beach with its hotels, where

" His humid front the cive, anheling, wipes,"

and wanders smiling on " ventiferous ripes."

Neighbors of Holmes at Beverly Farms are John T. Morse, Henry Lee, Robert Rantoul, and others. His own residence is quite near the depot, and is a plain, cream-colored house, with green blinds and broad front verandah and surrounding yard and apple orchard, — a house conspicuous for its plainness, in contrast with the magnificent villas that crown the rocky, wooded crags, and peep castle-like from the verdure. There is a good bathing-beach, from which, on a breezy day, you may see the far snow-spray tossing above the rocks and islands that line the coast, — Eagle

Island, Misery Island, Marblehead Rock, etc. Besides the owners of the villas, there is a small "native" population.   They have a collection of books, with a cosey name painted on a quaint little sign above the door: "The Neighbors' Library."   Mrs. Sargent's rooms are very pleasantly and tastefully decorated — old-fashioned fire-places, chintz-covered furniture, Japanese wall hangings, etc.   At Beverly Dr. Holmes drives out frequently with his wife, on pleasant days, and on such occasions may often be heard composing his poems *al fresco*, — testing them by the open air, as Whitman advises.

In the autumn of 1882 Dr. Holmes resigned his position as Parkman Professor of Anatomy in Harvard University, — a position which he had held for thirty-five years.   His chief reason, as announced, was that he might devote himself more particularly to literary pursuits, — especially to writing for the *Atlantic Monthly* magazine.   Upon laying aside the professor's gown to enjoy a little well-earned leisure, he was immediately appointed by the college Professor Emeritus, and his vacant chair will be filled by Dr. Thomas

Dwight, a fellow-teacher in the Medical School.

On Tuesday, November 28, Dr. Holmes delivered his last lecture before his students. The amphitheatre of the anatomical lecture-room was packed with students, and many gray-haired practitioners were present, assembled to hear their old teacher for the last time in that capacity. As the Doctor entered the room the audience rose to their feet with acclamations, and when the applause ceased one of the students presented him, in behalf of his last class, with a beautiful "Loving-Cup," inscribed with the following quotation from one of his own poems: "Love bless thee, joy crown thee, God speed thy career." This proof of the esteem in which he was held by his pupils was almost too much for the Professor's quick emotional nature. As soon as he had got control of the springs of feeling he began his address, which was naturally retrospective, passing in review his long connection with the school, with references to his early college days, and some account of the teachers and associates of his youth, of his studies at the Ecole de Médecine, La Charité, Hôtel Dieu, and the Invalides, in Paris, and of the noted physicians whom he heard lecture in that city, — Baron Boyer, Baron Larrey (Napoleon's favorite surgeon), Baron Dupuytren, Lisfranc, Velpeau, Broussais, Gabriel Andral, and, above all, Pierre Charles Alexandre Louis, by whom Holmes and his fellow-students were ready to swear at all times, and who exercised more influence on them than any of the other living masters in the science. There are in this lecture of Dr. Holmes some strong, nervous portraitures of those grim French *savans*, — Larrey, the short, square, substantial man, with iron-gray hair, red face, and white apron ; Dupuytren, oracular, Websterian, dominating ; Lisfranc, who used occasionally, when a phlebotomizing fit was on him, to order a wholesale bleeding of his patients, right and left, whatever was the matter with them, and who was heard one day lamenting the splendid guardsmen of the old empire because they had such magnificent thighs to amputate ! Then there was Velpeau, who walked to Paris in wooden shoes and worked his way up to eminence ; Brous-

sais — ("the way in which that knotty-feat-
ured, savage old man would bring out the
word *irritation* — with rattling and rolling re-
duplication of the resonant letter *r* — might
have taught a lesson in articulation to Sal-
vini"); and finally Louis, of whom his students learned the great truth, — afterwards
enforced in this country by Dr. James Bigelow and Dr. Holmes himself, — that a very
large proportion of diseases get well of themselves.

Having finished his "show of ghosts," as
he termed it, the lecturer made some practical
remarks on the way science was tending, and
some pleasantly sarcastic observations on
the old building where he had so long taught,
remarking that he had always thought it best
to abstain from anything like eloquence lest
a burst of too emphatic applause might land
himself and class in the cellar, alluding also
in a humorous way to the twilight region
under the amphitheatre, where he had for
years made preparations for his lectures.

In addition to the offering of the cup, a
beautiful basket of flowers was presented by
former pupils of the Doctor. In afterwards

acknowledging the cup by letter, he said that the unexpectedness of the tribute had made him speechless, but that he was sure that they did not mistake *aphasia* for *acardia*, and that his heart was in its right place though his tongue forgot its office. In the *Boston Medical and Surgical Journal* for December 7, 1882, will be found a complete report of this farewell lecture. It is also published in separate form.

This seems an appropriate place to mention that Dr. Holmes is a member of the Massachusetts Medical Society, President of the Boston Medical Library Association, and Vice-President of the American Academy of Arts and Sciences.

In person Holmes is a little under the medium height, though it does not strike you so when you see him, especially on the street, where he wears a tall silk hat and carries a cane. As a young man he was, like Longfellow, a good deal of an exquisite in dress; and he has always been very neat and careful in his attire. He is quick and nervous in his movements, and conveys, in speaking, the impression of energy and intense vitality;

and yet he has a poet's sensitiveness to noises, and a dread of persons of superabundant vitality and aggressiveness. When the fountain of laughter or smiles is stirred within him his face lights up with a winning expression and a laughing, kindly glance of the eye. When he warms up to a subject in conversation he is a very rapid, vivacious speaker. Hawthorne recorded his observation of this quality as early as 1843. In his " Hall of Fantasy " he describes certain poets whom he saw " talking in groups, with a liveliness of expression, or ready smile, and a light intellectual laughter, which showed how rapidly the shafts of wit were glancing to and fro among them. In the most vivacious of these," he says, " I recognized Holmes." Perhaps it is in his *vers d'occasion* and his after-dinner speeches that he has shone most brilliantly in society. At the breakfast given to him in New York city, in 1879, by the Rev. Dr. Henry C. Potter, Mr. George William Curtis, who, as all the world knows, is a very prince among impromptu and graceful speakers, aptly began his post-prandial remarks by the following little prologue (the poetical quotation being from one of Dr. Holmes' early poems) : —

> " ' I know it is a sin
>   For one to sit and grin
>   At him here ' —

But how can I help it ? How can any of us help it ? We have all been grinning for a generation, and my only comfort is that the whole English-reading world are our fellow-sinners. Indeed, for many a year, at happy little feasts like this, the chief dish — what the French with their incomparable and incomprehensible felicity call the piece of resistance, because, I suppose, nobody can resist it — has been a poem of his own, read by your distinguished guest."

Let us see also what impression he has made upon foreign visitors. . Chatty Miss Mitford said of him in 1851 : " He is a small, compact little man (says our mutual friend), the delight and ornament of every society he enters, buzzing about like a bee, or fluttering like a humming-bird, exceedingly difficult to catch, unless he be really wanted for some kind act, and then you are sure of him."

In 1875 Dr. Appleton, the Oxford scholar, met Holmes at the Saturday Club in Boston : —

"Dr. Holmes was highly talkative and agreeable; he converses very much like the Autocrat of the Breakfast-Table, — wittily, and in a literary way, but, perhaps, with too great an infusion of physiological and medical metaphor. He is a little deaf, and has a mouth like the beak of a bird ; indeed he is, with his small body and quick movements, very like a bird in his general aspect. When poor Kingsley was in Boston he met Holmes, who came in, frisked about, and talked incessantly, Kingsley intervening with a few words only occasionally. At last Holmes whisked himself away, saying, 'And now I must go.' 'He is an insp-sp-sp-ired j-j-j-h-ack-daw,' said Kingsley." [*]

Mr. David Macrae, a Scotchman, in his book called "The Americans at Home," [†] gives a lively picture of Holmes, the lecturer,

[*] Quoted by Mr. Sanborn in "Homes and Haunts of our Elder Poets."

[†] As quoted in William Shepard's "Pen Pictures of Modern Authors," pp. 147, 149.

as he saw him and heard him in 1863. The occasion was an inaugural address before the Medical School : —

"Holmes is a plain little dapper man, his short hair brushed down like a boy's, but turning gray now, a trifle of furzy hair under his ears ; a powerful jaw, and a thick, strong under-lip that gives decision to his look, with a dash of pertness. In conversation he is animated and cordial, — sharp, too, taking the word out of one's mouth. When Mr. Fields said, 'I sent the boy this — ' ' Yes ; I got them,' said Holmes.

" Dr. Holmes now gets up, steps forward to the high desk amidst loud cheers, puts his eye-glasses across his nose, arranges his manuscript, and, without any prelude, begins. The little man, in his dress-coat, stands very straight, a little stiff about the neck, as if he feels that he cannot afford to lose anything of his stature. He reads with a sharp, percussive articulation, is very deliberate and formal at first, but becomes more animated as he goes on. He would even gesticulate if the desk were not so high, for you see the arm that lies on the desk beside his manuscript

giving a nervous quiver at emphatic points.
The subject of this lecture is the spirit in
which medical students should go into their
work, — now as students, afterwards as prac-
tioners. He warns them against looking on
it as a mere lucrative employment. 'Don't
be like the man who said, "I suppose I *must*
go and earn that d—d guinea!"' He en-
livens his lecture with numerous jokes and
brilliant sallies of wit, and at every point
hitches up his head, looks through his glasses
at his audience as he finishes his sentence,
and then shuts his mouth pertly with his
under-lip, as if he said, 'There, laugh at
that!'"

CHAPTER VIII.

CHARACTERISTICS.

THE task of him who would, with however light a touch, give some analysis and interpretation of the writings of a loved and venerated author, now full of years and honors, and enshrined as a personal friend in the affections of thousands who have never even seen him in person, is indeed a delicate one. To avoid the error of the youthful newspaper critic administering his masterly rebukes to Homer, and Carlyle, and Emerson, and other presumptuous writers of like calibre, — to avoid this is not very difficult for one who has been mellowed a little by time, and taught caution by experience. But there is a class of persons who, in the case of a favorite author, take in a sort of dudgeon analysis of any sort, however respectful and delicate. These idolizers would fain persuade themselves that their hero has had conferred upon him a providential exemption from faults and deficiencies. Such persons had better skip this chapter. Then the hero himself, if he has been petted, is apt to take criticism with a wry face. It is unnecessary to say that this is not the case with Holmes, who in almost all of his writings is himself purely and distinctively a satirist, and for a lifetime has been lashing others with the most stinging and excoriating satire (tempered with humor and good-nature). Of course such a one would not stultify himself by asking exemption from good-humored retaliation ; indeed, he distinctly states somewhere in one of his Breakfast-Table talks that he welcomes criticism, because then he himself feels free to exercise his own gift in that direction. The really great man always welcomes the truth, if it is spoken in a generous and kindly spirit.*

* Compare the following from his paper entitled "The Autocrat gives a Breakfast to the Public" (*Atlantic Monthly*, December, 1858) : "Every man of sense has two ways of looking at himself. The first is an everyday working view, in which he makes the most of his gifts and accomplishments. It is the superficial stratum in which praise and blame find their sphere of action, — the region of comparisons, — the habitat where envy and jealousy are to be looked for. But

Broadly speaking, Holmes is Janus-faced, that is, he has a dual nature : he laughs on one side of his face, and is serious on the other ; in one mood, fun, humor, laughing satire predominate : he is a harlequin tumbling in mottled coat, a court fool bubbling over with puns and saucy jests, a Yorick, a Mercutio, and nimble-witted as they ; but suddenly some hidden spring of feeling or pathos is touched, the eyes brim with tears, and the soul soars upward in a rapt passion of tenderest sentiment. Presently the mood changes again, and deep-eyed Sorrow glides away veiled in tears and sable weeds, and Joy peers in through trellis of perfumed roses, and laughs to see her merry boy transformed to a sober, spectacled, dry-as-dust professor and scientist, delivering a learned lecture upon the processes and sutures of Yorick's skull, or

underneath this surface-soil lies another stratum of thought, where the tap-roots of the larger mental growths penetrate and find their nourishment. Out of this comes heroism in all its shapes; here the enterprises that overshadow half the planet, when full grown, lie, tender in their cotyledons. In this deeper region a man calmly judges and weighs his nature, and knows that the accident of applause is often but temporary."

the simian tendencies in the facial angle of Dick Turpin or Jack Newgate. Holmes is, on the one hand, a humorous poet and satirico-humorous essayist and novelist ; and, on the other, a lay-preacher, an earnest thinker, a cultured and accurate teacher, and an original scientific investigator. And yet these numerous endowments and traits are all blended in one homogeneous personality, — humor twining like a silver thread through the whole nature and gleaming out for a moment in the midst of the most serious disquisition or address ; and science in turn invading the poem, the novel, and the essay, and giving to these the solid value of accurate observation.

He is greatest as a humorist. As a writer of comic poetry he is excelled by no other English author. Hood's verses are slovenly in construction and not so gayly riant as Holmes', do not shake the diaphragm so deeply. In Holmes the essayist (when in his best moods) we have Swift without his rabid savagery, Sterne without his salaciousness, Steele without his shuffling irresolution, and Pope without his envenomed bitterness.

When at its best his humor has the genial
and kindly character which marks that of all
the great humorists; but too often it is only
an ironical smirk, a sardonical grin, a laughing *at* others instead of with them. The
comic in him is always saved from rodo-
montade and monstrosity by an equipoise of
shrewd practical sense: we tremble as his
glowing wheel grazes the brink of bombast
and folly, but with a cut of the lash, and a
short turn, away he flies again, laughing, and
we laughing with him.

As has been intimated, his finest humor
borders close upon pathos, and this is true
of Hood and Dickens; it is true of Gough
and Beecher, and of all great orators and
humorists. There is no well-defined line of
separation between the comic and the pathetic,
or tragic; the only difference being, as Scho-
penhauer points out, that the comic is purely
objective, and deals with the forms and sur-
faces of things, while the tragic is subjective,
dealing with the innermost nature and the
depths of life; but things that seem comic to
some are tragic to others, and *vice versa.*
"Humor! humor is the mistress of tears,"

says Thackeray : " she knows the way to the *fons lachrymarum*, strikes in dry and rugged places with her enchanting wand, and bids the fountain gush and sparkle. She has refreshed myriads more from her natural springs than ever tragedy has watered from her pompous old urn."

· There is much in Holmes that reminds one of dear foolish old Pepys. Like him he is sweetly sentimental about himself ; he is never done talking about himself, and especially about his childhood. The poetry of his early life clings and twines about his heart in perennial freshness and interest. All poets feel a certain sweet sting and poignant joy when recalling their childhood. The early life of Holmes was exceptionally happy, and with Chaucerian *naïveté* and delight the white-haired boy babbles about it in a style so gay and charming that you fairly hold your breath with suspense of interest, and wish for the thousand and one nights of Scheherezade to listen to him. He has also Pepys' hearty, sensuous enjoyment of life, — loves rowing, racing, trees, women, flowers, perfumes, and a well-furnished table. (Isn't it funny that Pepys -

could never make an entry in his diary without recording what he had for dinner, — that
cut of beef at the Boar's Head, or that roast
duck eaten at my Lord so and so's ?)   Holmes
has Pepys' rashness and impetuosity.   He
says somewhere that a gentleman will say yes
to a great many things without stopping to
think, while a mean, shabby fellow will look
suspicious and cautious and hesitate a long
while for fear of some disadvantage to himself.
This observation is true if not pressed too
hard ; but it also seems to show in Holmes
the rashness of a quick, generous nature that
acts before it thinks, and is sorry for it afterwards.   That Dr. Holmes has said many
things in the heat and flush of manhood
which he would now like to unsay he himself
has admitted, both in private conversation
and in the 1882 preface to the new edition
of the "Autocrat of the Breakfast-Table."
It is to his honor that he has frankly conceded this.   In concluding this parallelism
between Pepys and Holmes, one may add that
between Sir Thomas Browne, also, and his
American fellow-physician there is a good
deal in common, — for example, their love of
antiquarian studies.

Holmes is one of the last survivors of an illustrious group of writers who lived in an epoch of great intellectual brilliancy, — the era of Transcendentalism. He belongs to what may, perhaps, be known to posterity as the Concord School, the writers belonging to which have one and all based their intellectual creations upon the moral, and whether they have sung or lectured, or written fiction, have never failed to reveal the fact of their Puritan antecedents by deftly wreathing the lustrous flowers of their thought around some hidden sermon, some practical moralization, or some useful lesson in life. Holmes was brought up in a Calvinistic family, as many of us have been ; and we know what a grip the horrors and the fatalism of that theological scheme get upon the nature. The one persistent purpose running all through the prose writings of our author has been to attack the effete ecclesiasticism of the Calvinistic creed. Like Emerson and Parker and Whittier, he has been a knight-errant of the religious sentiment, taking a good deal of odium upon himself in times when it almost meant social ostracism to inveigh against the colossal devil whom good people had mistakenly exalted into the seat of their God.

We have said that Dr. Holmes is to be classed with the Transcendentalists of the Concord School in respect of the ethical character of his writings; but he is to be sharply distinguished from them in one cardinal point: they made little of conventional manners and behavior, and much of individuality, and they sternly challenged established customs: Holmes conforms in all except religion.

Great men are necessarily egotistic; but there are different varieties of egotism. That of Holmes has not, it must be admitted, any element of grandeur in it. He says in "The Poet at the Breakfast-Table" (at the close of a series of works by him) : —

"*Liberavi animam meam* (I have unburdened my mind). That is the meaning of my book and of my literary life." He has a feeling of relief in having got rid of the thoughts that were pressing for utterance, —that is all! There is in that statement the confession of his great limitation, namely, that all his thoughts revolve around himself, himself, himself, — reminding one of that satirical

piece of Poe's on Nosology, wherein the man
with the big nose continually talks of himself and his nose, his nose, his nose. With
the genius, it is, " Woe is me if I speak not ! "
He chisels, or paints, or writes to satisfy the
craving within him for ideal expression, and
to advance the interests of truth. A considerable part of Holmes' poetry was written beyond doubt from the point of view of the
genius, and there are many of his poetical
creations which are the expression of purest
genius of the ideal sort ; and his humorous
verses have also the stamp of a kind of genius.
But looking at his nature as a whole, and
apart from exceptional flights of imagination
(as in " The Chambered Nautilus "), we must
pronounce him devoid of that sublimated
essence called genius, at least that kind of
genius which Poe, and Burns, and Keats possessed. In sooth he is at just the opposite
pole of their genius : he is shrewd practicality
incarnate ; he is purely a man of the world,
a man of dress-coats, and white neckties,
and drawing-rooms, which your genius never
is ; he advises conformity to the world, is
horrified at unconventional things, which a

genius never is ; he abuses the great Richter,* which no genius ever has done, or ever will do ; he has little or no sympathy for down-trodden and inferior races, † but the one distinguishing feature of genius is its volcanic, undying hatred of oppression ; and, finally, hear his own words : " You know twenty men of talent who are making their way in the world ; you may perhaps know one man of genius, and very likely do not want to know any more. . . . It must have been a terrible thing to have a friend like Chatterton or Burns." Such is Holmes' opinion of genius. But what then ? Simply this, that if he is not a genius of the Poe stamp so much the better. We do not want our authors all Poes. If the genius of Holmes is not of the high transcendental sort, yet, after all, it is a species of genius, and of the finest carat in its kind.

* See his " After-Dinner Poem " (Phi Beta Kappa, 1843).

† See " Autocrat," Chapter III. : " In the conflict of two races our sympathies naturally go with the higher." We will do Professor Holmes the credit to believe that this is one of those paragraphs which he says he regrets having written.

Holmes is fond of puns and fantastic conceits, to the making of which considerable preparation has evidently been given; he repeats himself a good deal; he is well read, but has not, like Emerson, made a professional study of belles-lettres; he has studied the humanities at first hand in man himself. The one most charming feature of his printed and spoken conversation is that he establishes a relation of sympathy between himself and his readers, or listeners, by expressing for them those common, everyday thoughts that we all think, but rarely say. The central core of him is bravery, honesty, kindliness. The sunshine of his soul gleams out upon you so often that you forget the offensive egotism of the cit in the charm of the artless humor and tender sympathy of his nature.

He is indigenous; throws up New England subsoil as he ploughs; his homespun characters speak the native patois, and the whole tone of his writings is racily and unaffectedly Yankee. Only his personal spirit and point of view and his serious diction are British.

Dr. Storrs of Brooklyn once told how, when living in a small German town across the seas, the reading of the various instalments of the "Autocrat of the Breakfast-Table" as they appeared transported him as magically to New England scenes as the rubbing of a little powder in his hands transferred the magician of the "Arabian Nights" to distant lands.

In spite of his city life he knows how to observe nature closely and describe her poetically. Witness such passages as this :—

"The spendthrift crocus, bursting through the
    mould
Naked and shivering with his cup of gold.
Swelled with new life, the darkening elm on
    high
Prints her thick buds against the spotted sky."
Spring.

This prose description shows a sharp ear and eye: "The woods at first convey the impression of profound repose, and yet, if you watch their ways with open ear, you find the life which is in them is restless and nervous as that of a woman; the little twigs are crossing and twining and separating like slender fingers that cannot be still; the stray leaf is to be flattened into its place like a truant curl ; the limbs sway and twist, impatient of their constrained attitude ; and the rounded masses of foliage swell upward and subside from time to time with long soft sighs, and, it may be, the falling of a few raindrops which had lain hidden among the deeper shadows."

Those who would enjoy a treat in the way of nature-writing should read Dr. Holmes' two or three articles in the " Atlantic Almanac," if they can obtain a copy of that valuable annual. Here are two vignettes out of it by the pencil of Holmes :—

" The Indian corn is ripe, beautiful from the day it sprung out of the ground to the time of husking. First a little fountain of green blades, then a miniature sugar-cane, by and by lifting its stately spikes at the summit, alive with tremulous pendent anthers, then throwing out its green silken threads, each leading to the germ of a kernel, promise of the milky ear, at last offering the perfect product, so exquisitely enfolded by nature, outwardly in a coarse wrapper, then in substantial paper-like series of layers, then in a tissue as soft and delicate as a fairy's most intimate garment, and under this the white even rows, which are to harden into pearly, golden, or ruby grains.   .   .   .

"But here comes winter, savage as when he met the Pilgrims at Plymouth, Indian all over, his staff a naked splintery-hemlock, his robe torn from the backs of bears and bisons, and fringed with wampum of rattling icicles, turning the ground he treads to ringing iron, and, like a mighty sower, casting his snow far and wide, over all hills and valleys and plains."

There is one prominent feature of Dr. Holmes' writings over which one hardly knows whether to be amused or satirical. The vanity of it is so deliciously apparent that one would simply allude to it and pass it over in silence did it not occupy so very conspicuous a place in his writings, and if it were not certain that a good deal of mischief has been caused by it among silly people, and a good deal of pain among many worthy people.*

* Harriet Preston, for example. The writer's attention was called to this author's novel of " Aspendale " after his own strictures on this matter had been written, and he finds that she is even more severe than he is on

Reference is made to all that talk about "the quality," "men of family," the "Brahmin caste," "the sifted few," "we Boston folks"; and, *per contra*, all those sneering allusions to "the rural districts," "the unpaved districts," the "large-handed bumpkins," "the deep-rutted villages lying along the unsalted streams, "the ungloved," "the folks who can't pronounce view," "the red-handed, gloveless undergraduate of bucolic antecedents squirming in his corner," etc. What *is* to be done with a man who will write such a sentence as this: "Even provincial human nature sometimes has a touch of sublimity in it"? Nothing — except to laugh at him. When a man like Dr. Holmes can seriously ask that we make out of various little sectional peculiarities of pronunciation, dress, and manners, capital distinctions that shall decide the social worth and station of people, we can only — smile.

The "Autocrat of the Breakfast-Table"

the "snobbishness," as she calls it, of Dr. Holmes, in his treatment of "provincial" people, among whom were her own ancestors. See "Aspendale," pp. 139-155.

begins with "quality" talk, and "Elsie Venner" begins with it, and it crops out in all his other writings. In this matter of family and caste he is the most badly bitten man we know. This is the kind of class feeling that is dear to the British heart. Indeed, is it not barely possible that this non-American trait has unconsciously exercised its influence to a slight extent in procuring for Holmes the admiration of the English, so that in a recent issue of one of the great London papers it was editorially stated that no contemporary American writer except Lowell had so amused and instructed the insular mind as Holmes had done? And no wonder they breathe a sigh of gratification over his pages. For what with communists, and nihilists, and radical republicans in every country of Europe, including their own, they must find it difficult to discover an author of eminence who can be modern and mediæval in a breath. A man who is so conservative in his social philosophy is a godsend to a nation surfeited with the too refulgent democratic sunlight of Mirabeau, Hugo, Gambetta, Garibaldi, and others. "I go politically for *e* quality, and socially for *the* quality," says Holmes. *The quality!* why, this sounds like high-life-below-stairs talk. The reason why he goes for the quality he explains in the introductory chapter to "Elsie Venner." But it is almost wrong to take advantage of one who has unbosomed himself so naïvely to his own injury. But we must probe the matter a little further. When Holmes expresses profound commiseration for poor geniuses like Poe, for poor old maids, and for poor reformers; and when Emerson admits that he abhors a man with a good, loud, hearty stomachic laugh, why is it that we immediately take the part of the genius and the reformer, think with admiration of Theodore Parker's "glorious phalanx of old maids," and feel deep in our natures a perverse hunger for something gross and strong, — say a horse-laugh, or even an oath from a fisherman or a teamster? And when Holmes says : "It has happened hitherto, so far as my limited knowledge goes, that the President of the United States has always been what might be called in general terms a gentleman. But what if at some future time the choice of the people should fall upon one on

whom that lofty title could not by any stretch
of authority be bestowed,"—when we con-
template this appalling possibility, why do we
thank God that Abraham Lincoln was not a
"gentleman"?   Or when the laureate of
Boston, in his "Rhymed Lesson," gives to
the young men of the Mercantile Library
minute furnishing-store rules for dress (boots,
cravats, breastpins, shirts, etc.), why, in disgust at all this pettiness and artificiality, can
we think with complacency of an act of
Joaquin Miller, who (as the author was told by
a friend of that poet) got so nauseated with
artificiality one day in Boston that he went
down to the wharves, selected two of the
hungriest-looking men he could find, brought
them to the Parker House, and paid for their
dinners, solely for the pleasure of seeing a
genuine, unsophisticated act that should keep
him sane until he should get away from the
city?   Or when the Autocrat tells us of the
unparalleled heroism of the lady who, at a
social gathering, actually spoke to a "poor
social mendicant" who wore no shirt-collar,
had on black gloves, and flourished a red
bandanna handkerchief, — why is it that

(while admitting the possible heroism of the act, though such things are sometimes done for display) we still have a wayward feeling of amusement at the trepidations and panics of our good friends, the carpet-knights, and think with pleasure of Thoreau and his woodchuck cap; of Audubon in the great hotel at Niagara, with his rifle and tattered garb of skins, — Audubon, at that very moment honored by the crowned heads of Europe, and by the civilized world; or of Thomas De Quincey going to one of the highest social gatherings in Edinburgh dressed in ink-bespattered linen trousers, and an old coat buttoned up to his chin, and upon his feet shoes of felt over which the snow had sifted ; or, finally, of that magnificent young Greek-faced sailor, with waving hair, whom Dr. Holmes himself describes so enthusiastically in the "Poet at the Breakfast-Table"?

But how about this chryso-aristocracy over which such a to-do is made? Why, they are the most charming and inoffensive people in the world, — most of them, — and we are always disposed to hearty liking for their

sunny, urbane characters except when we are
reading such champions of them as Holmes.
To be sure there is one type of American
chryso-aristocrat that forms a not very agreeable spectacle.   Holmes aptly likens him to a
gull : —

> "A gentleman of leisure,
>   Less fleshed than feathered ; bagged you'll find
>   him such ;
> His virtue silence ; his employment pleasure ;
>   Not bad to look at, and not good for much."

In other words, a sort of negative, mollus-
cous creature who shuns the lion-hunts, ex-
ploring expeditions, and civil and military
employments of his more manly British
brother, — his only value to the world being
that he serves as a walking advertisement to
his tailor, and as a model of conventional
etiquette to the poor.   It is not, indeed, to
such as these that we yield the homage of
our admiration, but to those industrious,
cheery-faced, scholarly men of wealth and
position (often men of "old family" stock)
who are free from bourgeois insolence of manner, are courteous, urbane, public-spirited,

in short, the men to add the required element of dignity to democratic life, the men for your governors, mayors, bank-presidents, or foreign ambassadors.

We may sum up an unpleasant subject by saying that our genial author has expressed a great deal of truth in a very offensive way. He has said, has he not, things that had better have been left unsaid? There can be no doubt that certain portions of the writings of Holmes have helped more or less to increase that spirit of caste, and nervous, morbid conservatism and timidity which is paralyzing the spontaneous creative and imaginative genius of Boston. This is a hard thing to say; but, if true, it ought to be said. Every foot of land in Boston, and every other piece of property there, begins to decline in value the moment great men cease to be produced. Of what worth are your buildings and ships and streets if not animated by a soul, if not permeated by the glowing and untramelled spirit of creative energy and a sympathetic unitary life? The question is whether the creative instinct in Boston literature is to be crushed out by criticism and formalism, and

robust manliness by morbid æstheticism.
We stand in the midst of dead systems of
thought. The freshness and glory and mystery of the new will certainly never fill our
souls as long as we cherish a public sentiment which makes original character and
individuality subordinate to petty conventional manners and the accident of birth.
We laugh at that Philadelphia editor who
printed in his magazine a translation of
Edward Everett Hale's "Man Without a
Country," under the impression that it had
never before appeared in an English dress.*
Yet upon Boston has fallen the infinitely
deeper disgrace of suppressing by law the
writings of the most powerful poetical genius
in America. But it is never too late to re-
form. The remedy for a stagnant literary
life is a fresh study of nature, and bravery in
standing out against the ridicule of critics
and conventional conformers.

If it were not that the theological battles
which Holmes was fighting a quarter of a
century ago are now, as he himself has re-

* See Potter's *American Monthly* for December, 1881,
and January, 1882, p. 103.

cently said, all won and passed wholly by, it would be interesting to draw up a *Religio Medici*, extracting from his books the doctrines which he believes as well as those he has combated in so many places and on so many occasions. The existence of a score and more of Unitarian churches in Boston, and the fact that the best intellect of the city has for half a century been either Unitarian or purely theistic, have combined to throw what is usually called orthodoxy into the shade there. A Cambridge lady told the author that when she was a girl at school she was ridiculed for belonging to an orthodox church, — just as in the West a boy or girl might be ridiculed by a schoolmate for belonging to a Roman Catholic church.

In the University circles in which Dr. Holmes has moved since he was a young man at college, the absurdities of the prevalent popular creeds have always been the subject of quiet merriment. But Dr. Holmes' father was an orthodox, that is, a Calvinistic, divine. In this we have the key, have we not, to the son's life-long warfare against Calvinism. It was necessary for him to define himself in

order to escape ridicule, in order to escape
the imputation to himself of his father's creed.
Then, too, those who have been brought up
in the Calvinistic creed know how tenaciously
it interweaves itself with the mental fabric;
and perhaps, yes, doubtless, Dr. Holmes had
for many years to wage verbal war against his
childhood's creed in order to get wholly free
from it himself. The Devil is one of the most
difficult things to get rid of (and no joke).
Young Oliver appears to have been haunted
by this old anthropomorphic phantom all
through boyhood. He was troubled not only
by the Devil, but by devils. He says that
there were two things that somewhat diabol-
ized his imagination when a boy, that is, two
things that induced belief in a formidable incarnate fiend prowling about the neighborhood of his father's house seeking whom he
might devour. These were, first, certain
marks called the "Devil's Footsteps," con-
sisting of bare, sandy patches in the pastures
where no living thing would grow; and, second, a patched place on one of the college
dormitories said to have been made by the
Evil One when he burst violently through the

side of the room where some gay, dare-devil students were travestying one of the rites of the church. Other circumstances fostered the superstitious tendency developed by these two facts (so striking to a child's mind). There was a dark store-room, through the key-hole of which the boy dimly saw great heaps of furniture, which, to his vivid imagination and fearful gaze, seemed to have rushed in pell-mell and climbed upon each other's backs, and there remained in enchanted immobility. Then there were wild stories told by country servant-boys of dreams, apparitions, and death-signs, and of contracts written in blood, left out over night, and taken away by the arch-fiend to be filed away for future use. When one remembers that these stories were all ingrained in the nature, along with what were to him actual and awful religious verities, one sees reason enough for religious controversy in after-life, and for resentment against the creed that had stuffed his head with such nonsense.

But there were counter-actions and counter-irritants. He hints that the dogma of the Immaculate Conception early received a severe blow in his mind by a whispered story of a too common event.   And then there was the clerical element to frighten and repulse him. The Doctor's readers are familiar with his frequent home thrusts at the clergy.   He says in one place that when he was a child some jolly, benignant clergymen used to pass the Sunday at his father's house, and made the day seem almost like Thanksgiving.   But occasionally one of the undertaker stamp would come, and by his woebegone looks and wailing pessimistic tones make religion utterly distasteful to him.   One, especially, so twitted young Oliver with his blessings as a Christian child, whining about the " naked, black children, who, like the 'Little Vulgar Boy,' hadn't got no supper, and hadn't got no ma, and hadn't got no catechism (how I wished for the moment I was a little black boy !), that he did more in that one day to make me a heathen than he had ever done in a month to make a Christian out of an infant Hottentot." Evidently Oliver was not destined to die early and pious ; and his career as a Harvard student, and as a medical student in Boston and Paris, did not directly stimulate superstition.

But Dr. Holmes' admirers do not need to be told of the fact that he has a deeply religious nature, — he could not be a poet if he had not. He owns a pew in King's Chapel (Unitarian), and is a pretty regular attendant. His religion is, and has been, a liberal theism, Transcendentalism in fact, as many prose and poetical passages witness. In his seventieth year he wrote the following stanza in his exquisite poem " The Iron Gate ": —

" If word of mine another's gloom has brightened,
   Through my dumb lips the heaven-sent message came;
If hand of mine another's task has lightened,
   It felt the guidance that it dares not claim."

Section fifth of " The Professor at the Breakfast-Table " is almost wholly given up to theological discussion. A curious instance of the old anthropomorphic ways of studying nature is furnished by the Doctor's explanation of a certain little useless collar-bone which is found floating about in the shoulder of the cat. In 1857 Dr. Holmes held this view about it: that it is there not as a survival, but because " the Deity respects a normal type more than a practical fact," or utility. (From a paper on "The Mechanism of the Vital Actions," in the *North American Review* for July, 1857.)

As chairman of the Boston Unitarian Festival in 1877, Dr. Holmes summed up neatly the various theological views which he always has loved to combat : —

" May I, without committing any one but myself, enumerate a few of the stumbling-blocks which still stand in the way of some who have many sympathies with what is called the liberal school of thinkers?

" The notion of sin as a transferable object. As philanthrophy has ridded us of chattel slavery, so philosophy must rid us of chattel sin and all its logical consequences.

" The notion that what we call sin is anything else than inevitable, unless the Deity had seen fit to give every human being a perfect nature, and develop it by a perfect education.

" The oversight of the fact that all moral relations between man and his Maker are reciprocal, and must meet the approval of man's enlightened conscience before he can render true and heartfelt homage to the power that called him into being. And is not the greatest obligation to all eternity on the side of the greatest wisdom and the greatest power?

"The notion that the Father of mankind is subject to the absolute control of a certain malignant entity known under the false name of justice, or subject to any law such as would have made the father of the prodigal son meet him with an account-book and pack him off to jail, instead of welcoming him back and treating him to the fatted calf.

"The notion that useless suffering is in any sense a satisfaction for sin, and not simply an evil added to a previous one."

One of the most frequently urged themes of Holmes is the now commonly-accepted doctrine of the limited responsibility of the human mind, owing to inherited tendencies. This is the key-note of the brilliant Phi Beta Kappa lecture of 1870, entitled "Mechanism in Thought and Morals." In his review of Mr. Prosper Despine's three volumes on the psychology of crime (*Atlantic Monthly*, 1875, p. 466), he maintains that moral responsibility is limited, that the *worst* criminals are virtually almost moral idiots, and therefore the least responsible of all for crimes committed. Despine believes that such men should not be capitally punished, but be confined. Holmes suggests that these dangerous automata ought to be confined *before* their crimes are committed. If there is a tendency in Dr. Holmes to lean toward the doctrine of complete criminal automatism, it is never carried to the length of totally denying that we must hold criminals responsible for their deeds, but is cautiously kept within known and proved scientific limits. He especially frowns upon the theological idea that moral responsibility is transmissible, and says that " the inherited tendencies belong to the machinery for which the Sovereign Power alone is responsible. The misfortune of perverse instincts, which adhere to us as congenital inheritances, should go to our side of the account, if the books of heaven are kept, as the great church of Christendom maintains they are, by double entry."

In his tilt against Jonathan Edwards (lecture read at the Radical Club, and afterwards published in the *International Review* for

July, 1880), he says, that there is good reason to believe that there are persons who
are born more or less completely blind to
moral distinctions, just as some are born color-
blind. Yet "we have a sense of difficulty
overcome by effort in many acts of choice."
So that, if not free, we think that we are, and
this in itself constitutes a powerful motive.
"Our thinking ourselves free is the key to
our whole moral nature. *'Possumus quia
posse videmur.'*"

In the article just quoted Dr. Holmes
draws a detailed parallelism between Edwards
and Pascal, finding them to have much in
common. He says of Edwards that his
ancestors had listened to sermons so long
that he must have been born with scriptural
texts lying latent in his embryonic thinking-
marrow, as undeveloped pictures lurk in a
film of collodion. He also suggests that the
Northampton divine must have read that text
that mothers love so well, "Suffer little *vipers*
to come unto me, and forbid them not, for of
such is the kingdom of God."

One should not forget to add that the few
hymns of Dr. Holmes are much admired, and

that there are beautiful fragments of religious poetry scattered through his works. What a sweet and trustful spirit breathes through these lines, from " Wind-Clouds and Star-Drifts " ! —

" Thou wilt not hold in scorn the child who dares
　Look up to Thee, the Father, — dares to ask
　More than Thy wisdom answers. From Thy
　　　　hand
　The worlds were cast ; yet every leaflet claims
　From that same hand its little shining sphere
　Of starlit dew ; thine image the great sun,
　Girt with his mantle of tempestuous flame,
　Glares in mid heaven ; but to his noontide blaze
　The slender violet lifts its lidless eye,
　And from its splendor steals its fairest hue,
　Its sweetest perfume from his scorching fire."

CHAPTER IX.

POETRY.

" His the quaint trick to cram the pithy line
That cracks so crisply over bubbling wine."—
HOLMES.

IT is as a writer of humorous poetry that
Holmes excels. His non-humorous poems
are full of beautiful passages, as we shall
see ; but they are not, many of them, perfect
works of art like the others ; they have not
the same unique flavor of individuality. A
goodly proportion of his best comic and humorous pieces are *vers d'occasion*, written
to be read at banquets or before select com-
panies. From time immemorial wit has sea-
soned table-talk. A company at table assigns
by instinct the chief *rôle* to the wit or humorist. The three meals of a day are its
green oases, its sparkling poems. "The
Poet at the Breakfast-Table,"— the title was
well chosen. In the freshness and buoyancy
of the morning hour the fancy plays most

delicately and spontaneously, and the poet of
Beacon Street has transferred to the pages of
his prose and his poetry the vitality and intensity of spirits that the cup of coffee im-
parts. He also understands the soft illusory
enchantment of the chandelier, what time its
lustre mingles with the. faint waxy aroma
and flowery perfume of the banquet-room.)

When the critic approaches the post-cœnati-
cal and convivial poems of Holmes, he will
throw aside his quill, if he is not a fool, and
yield himself with others to the fun and riant
humor of the moment.* If he does anything,
he will long for an artist's brush to paint
some such scene as this : (no Deipnosophis-
tean Greek debauch, with wreaths and wine,
but) an ample breakfast-table in a high and
sunny room, the cheery crackle of blazing
wood in a spacious fireplace, the delicate
aroma of coffee gratefully inhaled (but you
can't paint that), a cultured and merry com-

* " I would go fifty miles on foot," says Yorick, " for I
have not a horse worth riding on, to kiss the hand of
that man whose generous heart will give up the reins
of his imagination into his author's hands, — be
pleased he knows not why, and cares not wherefore."

pany seated at the table, and at its head the genial face of one crowned

"With white roses in place of the red,"

whose tender-glancing eye is now moist with tears, and now gleaming with fun, and whose lips at one moment utter subtle and sententious truth, and at another bubble over with puns and rippling laughter, and jests which put the company into such a state of interior titillation and stomachic exhilaration of mood that the snowy table-cloth is momently in danger of amber stains from shaking cups. And upon the frieze of the room let there be a motley procession of figures, — weird Elsie, sweet Iris and the Little Gentleman hand in hand, the poor Tutor, roguish Benjamin Franklin, gaunt Silence Withers, wayward Myrtle, and honest Gridley, — with gargoyles and grotesques at intervals, a whizzing Comet, the immortal One-Hoss Shay at the moment of its dissolution, the Spectre Pig, and the pensive Oysterman, and for scroll-work a chain of spiral, pearly shells with purpled wings outspread.

After reading a dozen or more pages of the

neat Augustan couplets of Holmes' best *vers d'occasion*, packed and crammed with little *genre* images and neat concretes, you have the comfortable feeling of a man who has just despatched a dish of hickory-nuts cracked in halves, and intermingled with raisins, — the whole washed down with a *gläschen* of old sherry. Or you feel as if you had been at Mr. Aldrich's "Lunch" :—

> "A melon cut in thin delicious slices,
>   A cake that seemed mosaic-work in pieces,
>   Two china cups with golden tulips sunny,
>   And rich inside with chocolate like honey."

But not all of Dr. Holmes' memorial and anniversary productions, and verses kindly written by request, are of equal merit. Scores of them are nothing but rhymed rhetoric and sentiment, and should never have been printed at all except in newspapers. Their author has said of late that he would like to go over his poetry and cull out the best for a final edition. It is to be hoped that he may find time for this task. He has told us of the origin of many of his verses :—

‘ I’m a florist in verse, and what *would* people say,
  If I came to a banquet without my bouquet ”?

And in another place : —

> “ Here’s the cousin of a king, —
> Would I do the civil thing?
> Here’s the firstborn of a queen;
> Here’s a slant-eyed Mandarin.
>
> *Would* I polish off Japan?
> *Would* I greet this famous man,
> Prince or Prelate, Sheik or Shah?
> — Figaro çi and Figaro là ! ”

What was a kind-hearted man to do? Of course he complied: the verses were ground out somehow, — and what poet could ever resist the temptation to publish? It is almost impossible to impart by quotations the spirit and hilarity of the best of these *vers d’occasion:* there is a whet and stimulant in every line: the humor of them is interior, below the midriff, and penetrates the thick integument of care and gravity with a slow, delicious feeling that finally breaks out into uncontrollable laughter. Read the “Modest Request” for an illustration; or the “ Chanson without Music,” — a voluble polyglot medley

that almost takes one's breath away, resembling nothing so much as the tipsy music of
a bobolink, or the vocal pyrotechnics of the
Southern mocking-bird : —

> "You bid me sing, — can I forget
>   The classic ode of days gone by, —
> How belle Fifine and Jeune Lisette
>   Exclaimed, 'Anacreōn, gerōn ei'?
> 'Regardez donc,' those ladies said, —
>   'You're getting bald and wrinkled too :
> When summer's roses all are shed,
>   Love's nullum ite, voyez-vous!'
>
> In vain ce brave Anacreon's cry,
>   'Of Love alone my banjo sings'
> (Erōta mounon). 'Etiam si, —
>   Eh b'en?' replied the saucy things, —
> 'Go find a maid whose hair is gray,
>   And strike your lyre, — we sha'n't com-
>   plain ;
> But parce nobis, s'il vous plaît, —
>   Voilà Adolphe! Voilà Eugène!'
>
> .   .   .   .   .
>
> Ginōsko. Scio. Yes, I'm told
>   Some ancients like my rusty lay,
> As Grandpa Noah loved the old
>   Red-sandstone march of Jubal's day.

I used to carol like the birds,
   But time my wits has quite unfixed,
Et quoad verba, — for my words, —
   Ciel! Eheu! Whe-ew!—how they're mixed!"

Some of Holmes' best anniversary poems have been those for the Phi Beta Kappa. "Post-Prandial" is one of these, and its rare fun will not be understood by those who are ignorant of the circumstance that Wendell Phillips, who is a distant "connection" of Holmes, and Charles G. Leland (Hans Breitmann) both had public parts to perform on the occasion that gave rise to the poem. "Rip Van Winkle, M.D. — An after-dinner prescription taken by the Massachusetts Medical Society at their meeting, held May 25, 1870," is a capital piece of professional fun. It is full of sly thrusts at antiquated doctors. They are typified in the person of Rip Van Winkle (a grandson of Irving's hero), who goes to sleep with the request that he be awakened once a year for the doctors' meeting. Rip

   " Had, in fact, an ancient, mildewed air,
A long gray beard, a plenteous lack of hair, —

The musty look that always recommends
Your good old Doctor to his ailing friends.
— Talk of your science ! after all is said
There's nothing like a bare and shiny head ;
Age lends the graces that are sure to please ;
Folks want their Doctors mouldy, like their
    cheese."

Holmes was class poet at college, and he
has remained class poet all his life. Thirty-
seven of his class anniversary poems appear
in his complete poetical works. Some of
them are in his finest vein and are of general
interest. For example, " The Boys," written
in 1859 : —

" Has there any old fellow got mixed with the
    boys ?
  If there has, take him out without making a
    noise.
  Hang the Almanac's cheat, and the Catalogue's
    spite !
  Old Time is a liar ! We're twenty to-night !

  We're twenty ! We're twenty ! Who says we
    are more ?
  He's tipsy, — young jackanapes ! — show him
    the door !

'Gray temples at twenty?'—Yes! *white* if we
please;
Where the snowflakes fall thickest there's
nothing can freeze!

.   .   .   .   .

Then here's to our boyhood, its gold and its
gray!
The stars of its winter, the dews of its May!
And when we have done with our life-lasting
toys,
Dear Father, take care of thy children, THE
BOYS!"

"The Last Survivor" is one of those fine
pieces of imagined retrospect, or forecasting
of the future, which is so excellently done in
the "Epilogue to the Breakfast-Table Series."
"The Archbishop and Gil Blas" may serve
as the comic counterpart of "The Iron Gate,"
and could, one thinks, scarcely have been
written except by an old physician who had
himself been a keen observer of old men:—

"*Can you read as once you used to?* Well, the
printing is so bad,
No young folks' eyes can read it like the books
that once we had.

Are you quite as quick of hearing?   Please to
  say that once again.
Don't I use plain words, your Reverence?   Yes,
  I often use a cane,
But it's not because I need it, — no, I always
  liked a stick ;
And as one might lean upon it, 'tis as well it
  should be thick.
Oh, I'm smart, I'm spry, I'm lively, — I can
  walk, yes, that I can,
On the days I feel like walking, just as well as
  you, young man ! "

The exquisite elegiac poem on his classmate, Prof. Benjamin Peirce — that grand old
mathematician of lion aspect, whose very presence seemed a proof of immortality, — is
pitched in a lofty key, as the subject, indeed,
could not but inspire.   Two of the stanzas
may need a word of explanation : —

" To him the wandering stars revealed
  The secrets in their cradle sealed :
  The far-off, frozen sphere that swings
  Through ether, zoned with lucid rings ;

  The orb that rolls in dim eclipse
  Wide wheeling round its long ellipse, —
  His name Urania writes with these
  And stamps it on her Pleiades."

The reference here is to Prof. Peirce's calculations of the perturbations of Uranus about the time of the discovery of Neptune by Leverrier and Adams. "Peirce" (says Dr. Thomas Hill of Portland, ex-President of Harvard University) "showed that the discovery of Neptune was a happy accident; not that Leverrier's calculations had not been exact and wonderfully laborious, and deserving of the highest honor, but because there were, in fact, two very different solutions of the perturbations of Uranus possible. Leverrier had correctly calculated one, but the actual planet solved the other, and the actual planet and Leverrier's ideal one lay in the same direction from the earth *only* in 1846." A writer in the New York *Nation*, October 14, 1880, says: "When, in 1846, he [Peirce] announced in the American Academy that Galle's discovery of Neptune in the place predicted by Leverrier was a happy accident, the President, Edward Everett, 'hoped the announcement would not be made public; nothing could be more improbable than such a coincidence.' 'Yes,' replied Peirce, 'but it would be still more strange if there were an

error in my calculations'; a confident assertion which the lapse of time has vindicated."

The reader of Dr. Holmes' class poems may
like to know the full names of certain class-
mates to whose memory poems are dedicated.
The initials J. D. R. stand for Jacob D.
Russell; F. W. C. for Frederick William
Crocker; J. A. for Joseph Angier; and H. C.
M., H. S., J. K. W., respectively for Horatius
C. Merriam, Howard Sargent, and Josiah
Kendall Waite.

There are no very strongly marked epochs
in his poetical development; still his poetical
activity may be roughly divided into four
periods, each with characteristics of its own.
During the first period — from 1830 to 1849
— the greater portion of the best humorous
poems were written. From 1849 to 1857 —
or from the fortieth to the forty-eighth year of
the poet — he seems, as he himself has intimated, to have fallen into a sort of literary
lethargy, and there was scarcely a poem produced which takes rank with the work of other
periods in his life. There is scarcely a
humorous poem in this group; and only three
satirical ones which stick in one's memory,—

namely, "The Moral Bully," "The Old Man of the Sea," and "The Sweet Little Man." It is a curious coincidence that this barren period extends precisely over the period of his summerings at Pittsfield, and over his career as a lecturer. In 1857 came the *Atlantic Monthly;* and the first contributions of Holmes to its pages — prose and poetry — form the finest literary work of his life. The poems published in the "Autocrat" are of so uniformly high an order that one may consider them as forming a group by themselves (1857–1858). They include such famous pieces as "The Chambered Nautilus," "Latter-Day Warnings," "Æstivation," "The One-Hoss Shay," and "Ode for a Social Meeting." The period from 1858 to the present time is distinguished by a very much larger proportion than before of anniversary and memorial verses, and other *vers d'occasion*, and for a decided preponderance of serious over humorous poems.

His early humorous poetry (and his later also) is idiomatic, pitched in a conversational key, full of bright fancies, rippling laughter, crisp and sparkling rhythm, and pleases most in virtue of the use of familiar and homely objects placed in the most incongruous relations. But we are not going to be betrayed into an analysis of Dr. Holmes' *vers de société.* Rash would be the man who should attempt it; and he would get no thanks for his pains either. Nor shall his early humorous poems be quoted. There is but one way : you must buy his poetical works and read them, — read them and laugh, and find your moral atmosphere cleared, your breath freer, your digestion better, and your whole nature sunnier than before.

A feature of all his versification is its neatness, — no slovenly rhymes, no slipshod metres. And Pope himself never crammed more meaning into single lines and stanzas, which gleam with the polish and delicate finish of fresh-minted coins of gold. Where will you find greater condensation (outside of the writings of Tacitus) than in such lines as these : —

> " The sexton, stooping to the quivering floor
> *Till the great caldron spills its brassy roar,*
> Whirls the hot axle," etc.
>
> *The Bells.*

"These are the scenes: a boy appears;
  Set life's round dial in the sun,
Count the swift arc of seventy years,
  His frame is dust; his work is done."
                    Birthday of Daniel Webster.

"True to all truth the world denies,
  Not tongue-tied for its gilded sin;
Not always right in all men's eyes,
  But faithful to the light within."
A Birthday Tribute to James Freeman Clarke.

"Its irised ceiling rent, its sunless crypt unsealed."
                    The Chambered Nautilus.

"For these the blossom-sprinkled turf
  That floods the lonely graves
When Spring rolls in her sea-green surf
  In flowery-foaming waves."
                    The Two Armies.

There is still another whole compartment
in the mind of this many-sided man which we
have not explored, — his tender passion and
delicate feminine sensibility. Every person
of mature years who passed through the fiery
furnace of the American Civil War of 1861–65
came out chastened and purified and elevated

in nature. Already in 1861 we seem to see the influence of the opening war upon Holmes, in the prelude to his " Songs in Many Keys " (1861). After this his mind seems sobered and elevated to more earnest and impassioned poetical thought. But perhaps it is only the sobering influence of years that we notice. The key-note of the change is struck in the prelude just mentioned : —

" Song is thin air; our hearts' exulting play
  Beats time but to the tread of marching deeds,
  Following the mighty van that Freedom leads,
  Her glorious standard flaming to the day !
  The crimsoned pavement where a hero bleeds
  Breathes nobler lessons than the poet's lay.
  Strong arms, broad breasts, brave hearts, are
        better worth
  Than strains that sing the ravished echoes
        dumb."

The poem " Musa " is full of a youthful, rich, Oriental fire and passion that one had hardly suspected in Holmes, — reminds you of some of Bayard Taylor's poems of the East. So do the following two stanzas (" Fantasia ") : —

" Kiss mine eyelids, beauteous Morn,
  Blushing into life new-born !
  Lend me violets for my hair,
  And thy russet robe to wear,
  And thy ring of rosiest hue
  Set in drops of diamond dew !

  Kiss my cheek, thou noontide ray,
  From my Love so far away !
  Let thy splendor streaming down
  Turn its pallid lilies brown,
  Till its darkening shade reveal
  Where his passion pressed its seal ! "

"Under the Violets" has the delicacy of "Claribel," and all the artlessness of Herrick's pieces without their sensuality. "Iris, her Book," is full of that subtle, tremulous feeling, and sensitive psychical affinity which unlocks for its author the inmost souls of such young girls as Iris and Myrtle Hazard. A poet never hung more breathlessly over an opening lily, or gazed more reverently into the innocent little face of the spring's first violet, than the creator of Iris and Elsie has watched the Psyche unfolding in a young girl's nature, or new-born Eros trying his wings in the rosy light of her fancy.

One topic still remains to be touched upon, and we would not treat it in an ungracious or complaining spirit, — namely, the Anglicism of his poetical vehicle or metrical style. That this is not original does not detract from the merit of his poetry in the eyes of those who were partially nourished by the poetry of the Queen Anne school. He is a man of the world, a university man, and we should hardly expect such a one to strike out a new style in poetry, like the great lovers of nature, — Wordsworth, Burns, Emerson, Whitman : still it remains to inquire how the style of the Boileau and Pope school acquired such a life-long hold upon him. The answer is doubtless to be found in the circumstance that in his father's house, and in the university town where he lived as a youth, that species of poesy was exclusively fashionable at the time when his poetical style was forming. If there is a great deal in Holmes that reminds one of William Spencer, of Crabbe, Pope, Hood, and the Prize Poets of the English universities, —

it is because these were the popular poets when he was a boy and when he was in college. He tells us in the " Atlantic Almanac " that he and the other children of his father's house were educated on such English books as Miss Edgeworth's " Frank " and " Parent's Assistant," " Original Poems," " Evenings at Home," and " Cheap Repository Tracts," and says that he considers it to have been a great misfortune that they should have been fed on these English books instead of on American ones, for the former were full of words that had no meaning for them. They found themselves in a strange world where James was called " Jem," not Jim as they always heard it ; where a young woman was called " a stout wench " ; where the boys played, not at marbles, but at " taw "; where mischievous boys crawled through a gap in a hawthorn hedge to steal Farmer Giles' red-streaks, instead of shining over the fence to hook Daddy Jones' Baldwins ; where Hodge used to go to the ale-house to get his mug of beer, whereas they used to see old Joe steering for the grocery to get his glass of rum ; where toffy and lollypop were eaten in place of molasses-candy and gibraltars; where poachers were pulled up before the squire for knocking down hares with sticks, while to their knowledge boys hunted rabbits with guns, or set "figgery-fours" for them without fear of the constable; "where birds were taken with a wonderful substance they called bird-lime; where boys studied in *forms*, and where there were fags, and ushers, and barrings-out; where there were shepherds, and gypsies, and tinkers, and orange-women, who sold *China* oranges out of barrows; where there were larks and nightingales instead of yellow-birds and bobolinks." Upon all this the Doctor remarks: "What a mess, — there is no better word for it, — what a mess was made of it in our young minds in the attempt to reconcile what we read about with what we saw. It was like putting a picture of Regent's Park on one side of a stereoscope, and a picture of Boston Common on the other, and trying to make one of them. The end was that we all grew up with a mental squint that we could never get rid of."

How closely the heroics of Dr. Holmes

resemble those of Goldsmith and Pope no careful reader needs to be told. As for Hood, there is a striking resemblance between his features and those of Holmes, and there is a striking general resemblance between the style and literary methods of the two in some of their humorous poems. Holmes is unique and original in matter, only his style shows the influence of Hood. To show to what purpose Hood was read by Boston and Cambridge people about the time when Holmes was making his first poems, read the following stanza selected by the writer from many similar ones in the *Boston Daily Advertiser* for 1830. The verses are called " Fashionable Eclogues " : —

"Next year, papa ! next year, mamma !
　　You know I'm thirty-two,
(I call myself but twenty-six,
　　So this is *entre nous :*)
Next year I shall be thirty-three,
　　I've not a day to lose,
Oh, let us go to town at once,
　　I'm lost if you refuse."

Compare the metrical flow of this with
Hood's "Sally Simpkins' Lament" : —

> "Oh Jones, my dear! Oh dear! my Jones,
>   What is become of you?

> "Oh! Sally dear, it is too true, —
>   The half that you remark
> Is come to say my other half
>   Is bit off by a shark!

> "Oh! Sally, sharks do things by halves,
>   Yet most completely do!
> A bite in one place seems enough,
>   But I've been bit in two."

Hood's "Ode on a Distant Prospect of
Clapham Academy" contains just the touch
of Holmes in his "Old Cambridge."   Hood
says : —

> "Ay, that's the very house!   I know
>   Its ugly windows, ten a-row!
>   Its chimneys in the rear!
>   And there's the iron rod so high,
>   That drew the thunder from the sky
>   And turned our table-beer!

And Mrs. S——? Doth she abet
(Like Pallas in the parlor) yet
    Some favor'd two or three, —
The little Crichtons of the hour,
Her muffin-medals that devour,
    And swill her prize — bohea?"

And Holmes' metres run as follows : —

" The yellow meetin' house, — can you tell
Just where it stood before it fell,
    Prey of the vandal foe, —
Our dear old temple, loved so well,
    By ruthless hands laid low?
Where, tell me, was the Deacon's pew?
Whose hair was braided in a queue?
(For there were pig-tails not a few), —
    That's what I'd like to know."

So much for the metrical vehicle of Holmes,
and the models on which he formed his style.
A poet must choose some style or other, and
the Boston singer found that of the school of
Pope and Hood best fitted for his use. By
any other name the rose would smell as
sweet. In the case of humorous or comic
verse, we need not quarrel much with the
style, if the matter be but good.

Inasmuch as Dr. Holmes has not yet edited a selection of his best poems, the following anthology may be an acceptable guide for hurried readers ; and let it be premised that all the preludes of the poet are exquisite pieces of poetry and sentiment. The best poems, in the judgment of the writer, are these : — *

Old Ironsides ; The Last Leaf ; The Cambridge Churchyard ; My Aunt ; Evening by a Tailor ; The Dorchester Giant ; The Comet ; The Music Grinders ; The September Gale ; The Height of the Ridiculous ; On Lending a Punch-Bowl ; Nux Postcœnatica ; A Modest Request ; The Stethoscope Song ; The Meeting of the Dryads ; The Mysterious Visitor ; The Toadstool ; The Spectre Pig ; The Ballad of the Oysterman ; The Hot Season ; The Moral Bully ; The Old Man of the Sea ; The Sweet Little Man ; The Chambered Nautilus ; The Two Armies ; Musa ; A Parting Health ; Prologue ; Latter-Day Warnings ; A Good Time Going ; The Last Blossom ; Contentment ; Æs-

* The poems are given in the order in which they occur in the latest edition (1882), and may therefore be read consecutively and chronologically by referring to the table of contents of the poems.

tivation; The Deacon's Masterpiece, or The
Wonderful 'One-Hoss Shay'; Ode for a So-
cial Meeting; Under the Violets; Iris, her
Book; Aunt Tabitha; Epilogue to the Break-
fast-Table Series; The Old Man dreams; The
Boys; The Last Survivor; The Archbishop
and Gil Blas; Benjamin Peirce; Dorothy Q.;
The Organ-Blower; Rip Van Winkle, M. D.;
Chanson without Music; A Sea Dialogue;
Grandmother's Story of Bunker-Hill Battle;
Old Cambridge; How the Old Horse won the
Bet; The Iron Gate; My Aviary; For Whit-
tier's Seventieth Birthday; The Coming Era;
Post-Prandial.

CHAPTER X.

THE SCIENTIST.

An abler pen than that of the writer of these pages will doubtless at some future time treat of Dr. Holmes as physician, professor, and scientific specialist. In the mean time one may indicate the general features of his scientific work, and give in epitome the gist of his interesting studies and original researches.

His first original work was his Boylston prize dissertation on "Indigenous Intermittent Fever," or malaria (1837), a paper still valued by physicians. Following this was his treatise on "The Contagiousness of Puerperal Fever" (1843), concerning which he has said :—

"When, by the permission of Providence, I held up to the professional public the damnable facts connected with the conveyance of poison from one young mother's chamber to another's, — for doing which humble office I desire to be thankful that I have lived, though nothing else good should ever come of my life, — I had to bear the sneers of those whose position I had assailed, and, as I believe, have at last demolished, so that nothing but the ghosts of dead women stir among the ruins."

Dr. Holmes has experimented considerably in optics. The reader has already learned of his stereoscopical researches and invention. In Volume IV. of the Proceedings of the American Academy will be found a paper by Dr. Holmes on certain original optical experiments, to which he gives the name " Reflex Vision."

He has also done some original work in microscopy. The first microscope owned by him was one of Raspail's, purchased for him by his father from the Rev. Dr. John Prince, of Salem. After making many experiments in the construction of microscopes, Professor Holmes finally succeeded in inventing one which suited his wants. It is not only useful for class purposes, but is also good for ordinary use by the addition of a simple hinged platform and stage, also devised by him. Volume II. of the Proceedings of the American

Academy contains a communication from him " On the Use of Direct Light in Microscopical Researches," accompanied by a drawing of a horizontal microscopical apparatus invented by himself. As illustrating his scientific accuracy in microscopical investigations, one may quote his own words, as published in his address before the Boston Medical Library Association : —

"I do not pretend to hoist up the Bibliotheca Anatomica of Mangetus and spread it on my table every day. I do not get out my great Albinus before every lecture on the muscles, nor disturb the majestic repose of Vesalius every time I speak of the bones he has so admirably described and figured. But it does please me to read the first descriptions of parts to which the names of their discoverers, or those who have first described them, have become so joined that not even modern science can part them ; to listen to the talk. of my old volume, as Willis describes his circle, and Fallopius his aqueduct, and Varolius his bridge, and Eustachius his tube, and Monro his foramen, — all so well known to us in the human body ; it does please me to know the very words· in which Winslow described the opening which bears his name, and Glisson his capsule and De Graaf his vesicle; I am not content until I know in what language Harvey announced his discovery of the circulation, and how Spigelius made the liver his perpetual memorial, and Malpighi found a monument more enduring than brass in the corpuscles of the spleen and the kidney."

Homœopathy Dr. Holmes believes to be an arrant humbug. Now, if you put a humbug and Dr. Holmes in juxtaposition you are sure to have a lively fight. And whe-ew! (as he would say) haven't the homœopathists caught it though! They have, and they have writhed under the lash, as the numerous replicatory pamphlets prove. Read, and you shall see.

In 1842 he published his two brilliant lectures on "Homœopathy and its Kindred Delusions." They were originally delivered before the Boston Society for the Diffusion of Useful Knowledge.

The first lecture gives an account of four famous delusions: (1.) The Royal Cure of the King's Evil, or Scrofula; (2.) The Wea-

pon Ointment, and the Sympathetic Powder;
(3.) The Tar-water mania of Bishop Berkeley;
(4.) The Metallic Tractors, or Perkinsism.

The first of these, the King's Touch, is too well known to need explanation. The Weapon Ointment, or Unguentum Armarium, was believed to cure wounds by being applied to the weapon that produced the wound, and the Sympathetic Powder performed the same office if applied to the blood-stained garments of the injured person, although that person might be at a great distance from the garments themselves.

Amiable Bishop Berkeley believed that his tar-water, made by stirring a gallon of water with a quart of tar, and then decanting the clear water, was a specific for about all the diseases under the sun. "He was an illustrious man," says Dr. Holmes, "but he held two very odd opinions,—that tar-water was everything, and that the whole material universe was nothing." The Metallic Tractors (invented 1796) were two pieces of metal, one apparently iron and the other brass, about three inches long, blunt at one end and pointed at the other. The tractors were applied for the cure of various ills by being drawn lightly for about twenty minutes over the affected parts. They were the invention of Dr. Elisha Perkins, of Norwich, Connecticut. The Tractor delusion swept over America and Europe like wildfire, and as quickly subsided. Of course those various delusions are described and classed with homœopathy in order to show that in Dr. Holmes' opinion one is as much a piece of imposture as the others.

The second lecture treats of homœopathy directly. It is conceived and written in a vein of noble scorn, and the thought is poured out along the pages with a lucidity, pungency of satire, and cogent understatement that give to the performance the velocity and penetrating force of a cannon-shot. Dr. Holmes never wrote anything in clearer, purer style than this.

The three great principles of Hahnemann, the founder of homœopathy, are these, as Dr. Holmes puts them :—

(1.) Like cures like. That is, diseases are cured by agents capable of producing symptoms in healthy persons resembling those found in sick persons.

(2.) The efficacy of medicinal substances reduced to a wonderful degree of minuteness, or dilution.

(3.) Seven-eighths at least of all chronic diseases are produced by the existence in the system of psora, or the itch.

As to the first of these principles, Dr. Holmes says that there are a few cases in which an ill is cured by remedies producing similar symptoms; but that it is absurd to say, as Hahnemann did, that the homœopathic axiom is the sole law of nature in therapeutics.

As to the second principle: the ridiculousness of the claim that the one-trillionth of a drop of any drug can produce any effect whatever on the system he illustrates by supposing that the *whole* of a drop of chamomile were diluted, or minimized, to the degree which Hahnemann's disciples prescribe: the calculation proves that the single drop of chamomile would have to be diffused through ten thousand seas of alcohol as large as the Adriatic! And yet a few pellets moistened in such a dilution are said to cure the most terrible and fatal diseases!

The third principle of Hahnemann is dismissed as unworthy of consideration. Dr. Holmes shows that many of Hahnemann's quotations from ancient writers are garbled; that the cures asserted to be effected by homœopathic medicines are really cures of nature, the unconscious, invisible physician of life; and, finally, that many eminent physicians of Europe have fairly and repeatedly tested homœopathy, and found it a complete humbug.

He closes his lecture as follows : —

"Such is the pretended science of homœopathy, to which you are asked to trust your lives, and the lives of those dearest to you. A mingled mass of perverse ingenuity, of tinsel erudition, of imbecile credulity, and of artful misrepresentation, too often mingled in practice, if we may trust the authority of its founder, with heartless and shameless imposition. Because it is suffered so often to appeal unanswered to the public, because it has its journals, its patrons, its apostles, some are weak enough to suppose it can escape the inevitable doom of utter disgrace and oblivion. Not many years can pass away before the

same curiosity excited by one of Perkins'
tractors will be awakened at the sight of one
of the Infinitesmal Globules.   If it should
claim a longer existence, it can only be by
falling into the hands of the sordid wretches
who wring their bread from the cold grasp of
disease and death in the hovels of ignorant
poverty.

"As one humble member of a profession
that for more than two thousand years has
devoted itself to the best earthly interests of
mankind, always assailed and insulted from
without by such as are ignorant of its infinite
perplexities and labors, always striving in un-
equal contest with the hundred-armed giant
who walks in the noonday, and sleeps not in
the midnight, yet still toiling, not merely for
itself and the present moment, but for the
race and the future, I have lifted my voice
against this lifeless delusion, rolling its shape-
less bulk into the path of a noble science it
is too weak to strike or to injure."

These lectures naturally produced quite a
commotion in the enemy's camp, and there
were a number of pamphlet replies by Doctors Charles Neidhard, A. H. Okie, Robert

Wesselhoeft, and others. But they must have been rather uncertain and evasive, if we may judge all of them by that of Dr. Neidhard. He, however, scores one good point against our poet-doctor, when he says that he ought to have satisfied himself of the truth or falsity of homœopathy by actual and irrefutable experiments of his own.

To what has been quoted from Dr. Holmes' utterances upon homœopathy, we may add this: In his "Currents and Counter Currents," he says: "There is in some persons a singular inability to weigh the value of testimony; of which, I think, from a pretty careful examination of his books, Hahnemann affords the best specimen outside the walls of Bedlam." And again: Homœopathy means "that the sick are to be cured by poisons. *Similia similibus curantur* means exactly this. It is simply a theory of universal poisoning, nullified in practice by the infinitesimal contrivance." And in the *Atlantic Monthly* for December, 1857, he sums up the whole matter in such a compact and characteristic style that it would be too bad to abbreviate or rewrite his words: —

"Of course it has had a certain success. Its infinitesimal treatment being a nullity ; patients are never hurt by drugs, *when it is adhered to.* It pleases the imagination. It is image-worship, relic-wearing, holy-water sprinkling, transferred from the spiritual world to that of the body. Poets accept it ; sensitive and spiritual women become sisters of charity in its service. It does not offend the palate, and so spares the nursery those scenes of single combat in which infants were wont to yield at length to the pressure of the spoon and the imminence of asphyxia. It gives the ignorant, who have such an inveterate itch for dabbling in physics, a book and a doll's medicine-chest, and lets them play doctors and doctresses without fear of having to call in the coroner. And just so long as unskilful and untaught people cannot tell coincidences from cause and effect in medical practice, — which to do, the wise and experienced know how difficult ! — so long it will have plenty of 'facts' to fall back upon. Who can blame a man for being satisfied with the argument, 'I was ill, and am well, — great is Hahnemann !' Only this argument serves all impostors and impositions. It is not of much value, but it is irresistible, and therefore quackery is immortal."

Only three years after the foregoing lines were penned by Dr. Holmes he startled the physicians of Boston with almost as severe an attack upon the allopathists, with whom he had always classed himself, as had been his attack upon the homœopathists. It must have caused a sensation indeed when one who had always been sarcastic over almost all hygienic and medical innovations, suddenly turned squarely about and belabored his own coadjutors, the solemn conservators of the traditions of old-fashioned medical practice. His address by no means gives countenance to homœopathy in any shape, and yet a fairly deducible inference from it is that a modified homœopathic practice may not be much worse after all than an unmitigated allopathic practice. The address (styled " Currents and Counter Currents in Medical Science ") was delivered at the meeting in Boston of the Massachusetts Medical Society, May 30, 1860, and afterwards published in book form. Its vigorous onslaught upon the excessive use of drugs in medical practice startled the learned members into a precipitate resolution, "That the society disclaim all responsibility for the sentiments contained in this annual address." Yet it is safe to say that so much sound sense has rarely been compacted between the covers of a medical *brochure* as we find in this lecture of Dr. Holmes. It ought to, and doubtless will, mark a turning-point, an epoch, in the medical practice of Boston. We like the clear, unequivocal ring of these pages. We like to see the ripe wisdom of thirty years' medical study and practice drawn upon so fearlessly in the interests of truth. The following is an abstract of the work : —

The community, says Dr. Holmes, is overdosed. The best proof of it is that no families take so little medicine as the families of doctors (except those of apothecaries), and that old practitioners are more sparing in the use of medicines than are younger ones. The chief defect of the medical practice of the day is that it neglects causes and quarrels with effects. The popular belief is that sick persons must feed on noxious and disagreeable substances, and a physician who does not prescribe these is thought to be worth little. A Boston physician was called to see a man with a terribly sore mouth. On inquiry he found that he had been taking a box of mercury pills that he had picked up in the street, — his idea being that all pills were good for people. It is one of the superstitions of the medical practice that a coated tongue invariably shows that the stomach needs an evacuant. But the condition of the tongue is no guide to that of the stomach, which is covered with a different kind of epithelium, and furnished with entirely different secretions. "A silversmith will for a dollar make a small *hoe*, of solid silver, which will last for centuries, and will give a patient more comfort used for the removal of the accumulated epithelium and fungous growths which constitute the 'fur,' than many a prescription with a split-footed ℞ before it, addressed to the parts out of reach." The Doctor says he thinks more of this little tool, because the use of it, or something like it, saved the Plymouth Colony in 1623, when

Edward Winslow, in attending the sick Indian, Massasoit, *scraped his tongue* and gave him such other treatment as insured his recovery and procured his gratitude to the extent of his revealing the Indian plot for the annihilation of the colony.

Speaking of the too great trust of the eminent Dr. Benjamin Rush in powerful and hasty remedies, our author says: " How could a people which has a revolution once in four years, which has contrived the bowie-knife and the revolver, which has chewed the juice out of all the superlatives in the language in Fourth of July orations, and so used up its epithets in the rhetoric of abuse, that it takes two great quarto dictionaries to supply the demand; which insists in sending out yachts and horses and boys to out-sail, out-fight, and checkmate all the rest of creation — how could such a people be content with any but 'heroic' practice ? What wonder that the stars and stripes wave over doses of ninety grains of sulphate of quinine, and that the American eagle screams with delight to see three drachms of calomel given at a single mouthful ? "

All noxious medicines and appliances which are not natural food or stimulants drain from the patient, we will say, five per cent of his vital force, and " in the game of life-or-death, *rouge et noir*, as played between the doctor and the sexton, this five per cent., this certain small injury entering into the chances, is clearly the sexton's perquisite for keeping the green table over which the game is played, and where he hoards up his gains."

Throw out opium, says Dr. Holmes; throw out a few specifics which a physician is hardly needed to apply ; throw out wine, which is a food, and the vapors of ether producing anæsthesia, and then sink the whole materia medica, *as now used*, to the bottom of the sea ; the result would be all the better for mankind, and all the worse for the fishes. In a note the Doctor adds that by this startling assertion " no denunciation of drugs as sparingly employed by a wise physician was or is intended ; but reference was had to the too abundant and injudicious use of such drugs as antimony, strychnine, acetate of lead, aloes, aconite, lobelia, lapis infernalis, stercus diaboli, tormentilla, and other such remedies.

Holmes has expressed decided opinions on some other much-debated subjects besides theories of medical practice. In the *North American Review* for July, 1857, will be found a review by him of certain physiological works by Draper, Carpenter, Grove, and Metcalfe, in which the then newly-emerging doctrines of evolution curiously jostle the old anthropomorphisms. The reviewer lays his hand on his heart, and makes many profound salaams to God, but keeps slyly thrusting him farther and farther back into the deeps of space to let the secondary forces do the main business of creation.

After disposing of the theological aspect of his subject by expressing his belief in an immanent deity, and quoting approvingly Oken's dictum, "The Universe is God rotating," he enters upon a discussion of the question of the existence or non-existence of a special creative vital force. He takes the negative view, and in a cogent and solid review of the correlation of forces, and of the whole field of organic life, reaches the conclusion that as pre-existing materials were employed to form organic structures, so pre-existing force or forces must have been employed to maintain organic actions, or unconscious life; that life is as necessary an attribute of a perfect organism as gravity is of metal, or hardness of a diamond; that, in short, there is almost a complete parallelism between the mechanism of vital phenomena and the mechanism of unvital phenomena. There is a strong probability that all forces (including, perhaps, matter as a force) are only different manifestations of one infinite incomprehensible force. Such a view simplifies our thinking, and satisfies the generalizing instinct. "Science is the art of packing knowledge."

Through Holmes' brilliant Phi Beta Kappa lecture on "Mechanism in Thought and Morals" run two richly illustrated thoughts, namely, that the brain contains a material, hieroglyphic record of thought; and, secondly, that this material and transmissible record is not incompatible with freedom of willing in the sphere of morals, although for certain great classes of actions men are not responsible.

There are some charming reminiscences

and antiquarian sketches by Holmes, to deprive the reader of some account of which would be an injustice. Among the Winthrop papers was discovered a manuscript written about 1643, and labelled " Receipts to cure Various Disorders." The receipts are signed Edward Stafford. Here is one of them as deciphered by Dr. Holmes, and given by him in the Proceedings of the Massachusetts Historical Society for February, 1862 :—

" *My Black powder against ye plague, small pox : purples, all sorts of feavers : Poyson ; either by Way of prevention, or after Infection.* In the Moneth of March take Toades, as many as you will, alive ; putt them into an Earthen pott, so y^t it be halfe full ; Cover it with a broad tyle or Iron plate ; then overwhelme the pott, so y^t ye bottome may be uppermost : putt charcoales round about it and over it, and in the open ayre, not in an house, sett it on fire and lett it burne out and extinguish of it self : When it is cold, take out the toades ; and in an Iron-morter pound them very well, and searce them : then in a Crucible calcine them so againe : pound and searce them againe. The first time, they will be a browne powder, the next time black. Of this you may give a dragme in a Vehiculum (or drinke) Inwardly in any Infection taken ; and let them sweat upon it in their bedds."

In illustration of this remarkable recipe, and of the old and still-existing superstition that the toad is poisonous, Dr. Holmes refers to the story in Boccaccio of "Pasquino and Simona," lovers, who perish by rubbing their teeth with the leaves of a sage bush. When the bush is plucked up by the roots, lo! a toad, to the poisonous qualities of which the death of the lovers is ascribed. That the toad has some unpleasant bodily peculiarities, the Doctor says he became convinced from an accident that happened once to a young puppy in his presence. The puppy was amusing himself by pushing a toad about with his nose, when suddenly he withdrew with marks of the most extreme disgust, and was at once attacked by such salivation as the Doctor had never seen before in man or beast. The dog never meddled with a toad again as long as he lived.

In giving some account of venerable Dr. Edward Augustus Holyoke (1728–1829) in the fourth volume of the Memorial History of Boston, Dr. Holmes tells a little incident concerning him.   He says that he one day took a student just beginning his medical education with him, — young James Jackson, — into the room where he kept his medicines. Pointing to the drawers and bottles ranged around the room, he said to the young man : "I seem to have here a great number and variety of medicines; but I may name four which are of more importance than all the rest put together, namely, Mercury, Antimony, Opium, and Peruvian Bark."   This worthy old centenarian had a great antipathy to cigars, as the following verses of his witness : —

<blockquote>

"And smoaked segars!
Vile substitute for that white, slender tube
Our fathers erst enjoy'd, in winter's eve,
When the facetious jest, or funny pun,
Or tales of olden time, or Salem witch,
Or quaint conundrum round the genial fire
The social hour beguil'd."

</blockquote>

Under the heading "Personal Recollections of Noted Physicians," Dr. Holmes notices, among Cambridge doctors, picturesque old Benjamin Waterhouse, with his "pyramid of titles of great dimensions," and famous for his introduction of vaccination in the Western World. Dr. Waterhouse vaccinated a great many persons, including the young Holmes, who afterwards described him as a brisk, dapper old gentleman, with hair tied in a ribbon behind, marching smartly about with his gold-headed cane, and upon his face a look of sagacity and oracular gravity. Lowell gives a delicious bit of description to fill out the picture : —

" His queue, slender and tapering, like the tail of a violet crab, held out horizontally by the high collar of his shepherd's-gray overcoat, whose style was of the latest when he studied at Leyden in his hot youth. . . . He wore amazing spectacles fit to transmit no smaller image than the page of mightiest folios of Dioscorides or Hercules de Saxonia, and rising full-disked upon the beholder like those prodigies of two moons at once, portending change to monarchs. The great collar disallowing any independent rotation of the head, I remember he used to turn his whole person in order to bring their *foci* to bear upon an object. One can fancy that terrified Nature would have yielded up her secrets at once without cross-examination, at their first glare."

Dr. Waterhouse's granddaughters still occupy his quaint old cottage in Cambridge, and the writer was told by them that half a century ago he had a great botanical garden in the rear of the cottage, where, like Dr. Rappaccini, he was wont to walk and hold converse with his plants. It was he who was instrumental in founding the Harvard College Botanical Garden (remembering the fragrant garden of this kind he had known at Leyden). Mr John Owen once told the writer of these pages an amusing anecdote of Dr. Waterhouse. Mr. Owen, being then a publisher in Cambridge, had provided a newspaper-room in the rear of his book-shop for the convenience of himself and his customers. One day Dr. Waterhouse came in, and Mr. Owen, accosting him, politely informed him that he would be happy to offer him the use of his reading-room gratis. The fiery little doctor looked at him a moment with his keen eyes, and then said slowly and with a pause between each word : " Melasses — is good — to ketch — flies !" But this has nothing to do with an account of the life and writings of Dr. Oliver Wendell Holmes, you say. True, it is a digression. But "digressions," says Yorick, " incontestably are the sunshine, they are the life, the soul of reading. Take them out of a book and one cold, eternal winter would reign in every page of it."

CHAPTER XI.

AUTOCRATIANA.*

THE INDIAN.

An Indian is a few instincts on legs, and holding a tomahawk.

READ "DON QUIXOTE."

When Sydenham was asked by Sir Richard Blackmore as to what medical books he should read, the answer was, "Read 'Don Quixote.'"

ILLUSION.

There is nothing as real in this world as illusion. All other things may desert a man, but this fair angel never leaves him. She holds a star a billion miles over a baby's head, and laughs to see him clawing and batting himself as he tries to reach it.

* In this chapter are collected a number of brilliant paragraphs and *mots*, mostly gathered out of fugitive or uncopyrighted publications of Holmes.

THE ÆOLIAN ATTACHMENT.

In a letter of Dr. Holmes', read at the Centennial Dinner of the Massachusetts Medical Society, we find a Holmes *mot :* —

If a doctor has the luck to find out a new malady, it is tied to his name like a tin kettle to a dog's tail, and he goes clattering down the highway of fame to posterity with his æolian attachment following at his heels.

CRITICISM.

If anything pleasant should be said about "the new edition," you may snip it out of the papers and save it for me. If contrary opinions are expressed, be so good as *not* to mark with brackets, carefully envelop, and send to me, as is the custom of many friends. —*Preface to 1848 edition of Poems.*

OLD WINE IN NEW BOTTLES.

As the wine of old vintages is gently. decanted out of its cobwebbed bottles with their rotten corks, into clean new receptacles, so the wealth of the New World is quietly emptying many of the libraries and galleries of the

Old World into its newly-formed collections
and newly-raised edifices.

INVALIDISM.

Invalidism is the normal state of many
organizations. It can be changed to disease,
but never to absolute health by medicinal
appliances. There are many ladies, ancient
and recent, who are perpetually taking remedies for irremediable pains and aches. They
ought to have headaches and back-aches and
stomach-aches; they are not well if they
do not have them. To expect them to live
without frequent twinges is like expecting
a doctor's old chaise to go without creaking; if it did, we might be sure the springs
were broken.

EX NIHILO NIHIL FIT.

Ex nihilo nihil fit. Given a half-starved
dyspeptic and a bloodless negative blonde as
parents, Hercules or Apollo is an impossibility in their progeny, yet people look
with infinite expectations of health, strength,
beauty, intellect, as the product of 0×-1.

OUR MORAL EXUVIÆ.

Is there no outlawry of an obsolete self-determination? If the president of the Society for the Prevention of Cruelty to Animals impaled a fly on a pin when he was ten years old, is it to stand against him, crying for a stake through his body, *in saecula saeculorum?* In Swedenborg's heaven, "*what we are* will determine the company we are to keep, and not the avoirdupois weight of our moral exuviæ, strapped on our shoulders like a porter's burden."

GUNPOWDER.

Chemistry seals up a few dark grains in iron vases, and lo! at the touch of a single spark, rises in smoke and flame a mighty Afrit with a voice like thunder and an arm that shatters like an earthquake.

APPLIED SCIENCE.

Science and art have in our time so changed the aspect of everyday life that one of a certain age might well believe himself on another planet or in another stage of existence. The wand of Prometheus is in our match-boxes ;

the rock of Horeb gushes forth its streams
in our dressing-rooms ; the carpet of Arabian
story is spread in our Pullman car ; our words
flash from continent to continent ; our very
accents are transmitted from city to city ;
the elements of forming worlds are analyzed
in our laboratories ; and, most wonderful and
significant of all, the despotic authority of
tradition is unsceptred since the angel of
anæsthesia has lifted from womanhood the
burden of the primal malediction.

EUTHANASIA.

That *euthanasia,* often accorded by nature,
sometimes prevented by want of harmony in
the hesitating and awkwardly delaying func-
tions, not rarely disturbed by intrusive influ-
ences, is a right of civilized humanity. The
anæsthetics mercifully granted to a world
grown sensitive in proportion to its culture
will never have fulfilled their beneficent purpose until they have done for the scythe of
death what they have done for the knife of
the surgeon and the sharper trial hour of
woman.

THE SCHOLAR AND HIS BOOKS.

The scholar's mind is furnished with shelves like his library. Each book knows its place in the brain as well as against the wall or in the alcove. His consciousness is doubled by the books which encircle him, as the trees that surround a lake repeat themselves in its unruffled waters. Men talk of the nerve that runs to the pocket, but one who loves his books, and has lived long with them, has a nervous filament which runs from his sensorium to every one of them.

TRANSLATION.

The translation of a poem from one language to another is in one sense an impossibility, — as much as it is to get a ripe peach from New Jersey to Boston; to carry a full-blown rose from here to San Francisco; to waft the salt-sea odor of Nahant from here to St. Louis.

THE UNKNOWN.

Science is the topography of ignorance. From a few elevated points we triangulate vast spaces, enclosing infinite unknown details.   We cast the lead, and draw up a little sand from abysses we shall never reach with our dredges.

THE POOH-POOHS.

The Pi-Utes and the Kickapoos of the wilderness are hard to reason with.   But there is another tribe of irreclaimables, living in much larger wigwams and having all the look of civilized people, which is quite as intractable to the teachings of a new philosophy that upsets their ancestral totems.   This is the tribe of the Pooh-Poohs, so called from the leading expression of their vocabulary, which furnishes them a short and easy method of disposing of all novel doctrines, discoveries, and inventions of a character to interfere with their preconceived notions.

SLANG.

The use of *slang*, or cheap generic terms, as a substitute for differentiated specific expressions, is at once a sign and a cause of mental atrophy.   It is the way in which a lazy adult shifts the trouble of finding any exact meaning in his (or her) conversation on the other party. If both talkers are indolent, all their talk lapses into the vague generalities of early childhood, with the disadvantage of a vulgar phraseology. It is a prevalent social vice of the time, as it has been of times that are past.

UNPREMEDITATED CRITICISM.

In Mrs. John T. Sargent's "Sketches and Reminiscences of the Radical Club," Dr. Holmes is recorded as saying that, when he was invited to speak without preparation on a carefully written essay, he always felt as he should if, at a chemical lecture, somebody should pass around a precipitate, and when the mixture had become turbid, should request him to give his opinion on it; besides, he added, the fallacies constantly arising in such a discussion from the lack of a proper definition of terms, always made him feel as if quicksilver had been substituted for the ordinary silver of speech. He declared that he preferred to take the essay home, slowly assimilate it, and not talk about it until it had become a part of himself.

INDIAN SUMMER.

To those who know the "Indian Summer" of our Northern States it is needless to describe the influence it exerts on the senses and the soul. The stillness of the landscape in that beautiful time is as if the planet were *sleeping*, like a top, before it begins to rock with the storms of autumn. All natures seem to find themselves more truly in its light; love grows more tender, religion more spiritual, memory sees farther back into the past, grief revisits its mossy marbles, the poet harvests the ripe thoughts which he will tie in sheaves of verse by his winter fireside.

THE SPIRAL COROLLA.

Look at the flower of a morning-glory the evening before the dawn which is to see it unfold. The delicate petals are twisted into a spiral, which at the appointed hour, when the sunlight touches the hidden springs of its life, will uncoil itself and let the day into the chamber of its virgin heart. But the spiral must unwind by its own law, and the hand that shall try to hasten the process will only spoil the blossom which would have expanded in symmetrical beauty under the rosy fingers of morning.

THE TWENTY-SEVENTH LETTER OF THE ALPHABET.

In 1879 the *Indianapolis News* published the following amusing note of the Autocrat, addressed to a young Quaker lady who had inquired about the twenty-seventh letter of the alphabet mentioned in " Elsie Venner " :

BOSTON, March 4, 1861.

MY DEAR MISS LAVINIA, — The twenty-seventh letter of the alphabet is pronounced by applying the lips of the person speaking it to the cheek of a friend, and puckering and parting the same with a peculiar explosive sound. " Cousin Edward " will show you how to speak this labial consonant, no doubt, and allow you to show your proficiency by practising it with your lips against his cheek. For further information you had better consult your gra'm'ma.   Very truly yours,

O. W. HOLMES.

P. S. — Are you any relation to "the lovely young Lavinia " who " once had friends," mentioned by Thomson in his " Seasons " ?

A STRONG SMELL OF TURPENTINE.

I once inhaled a pretty full dose of ether
with the determination to put on record, at
the earliest moment of regaining consciousness, the thought I should find uppermost in
my mind.   The mighty music of the tri-
umphal march into nothingness reverberated
through my brain, and filled me with a sense
of infinite possibilities, which made me an
archangel for the moment.   The veil of eternity was lifted.   The one great truth which
underlies all human experience, and is the
key to all the mysteries that philosophy has
sought in vain to solve, flashed upon me in a
sudden revelation.   Henceforth all was clear ;
a few words had lifted my intelligence to the
level of the knowledge of the cherubim.   As
my natural condition returned, I remembered
my resolution ; and staggering to my desk,
I wrote, in ill-shaped, straggling characters,
the all-embracing truth still gleaming in my
consciousness.   The words were these (children may smile ; the wise will ponder) : " *A
strong smell of turpentine prevails through-*

out."   [A narrow escape, Doctor! what if it had been sulphur?]

MUTUAL UNDERVALUATION.

I was passing through a somewhat obscure street at the west end of our city a year or two since when my attention was attracted to a narrow court by a sound of voices and a small crowd of listeners. From two open windows on the opposite sides of the court projected the heads and a considerable portion of the persons, of two of the female sex, — natives, both of them, apparently, of the green isle, famous for shamrocks and shillalahs. They were engaged in argument, if that is argument in which each of the two parties develops his argument without the least regard to what the other is at the same time saying. The question involved was the personal, social, moral, and, in short, total standing and merit of the two controversialists and their respective families. But the strange phenomenon was this: The two women, as if by preconcerted agreement, like two instruments playing a tune in unison, were pouring forth simultaneously a calm, steady, smooth-flowing stream of mutua. undervaluation, to apply a mild phrase to it; never stopping for punctuation, and barely giving themselves time to get breath between its long-drawn clauses. The dialogue included every conceivable taunt which might rouse the fury of a sensitive mother of a family, whose allegiance to her lord, and pride in her offspring, were points which it displeased her to have lightly handled. I stood and listened like the quiet groups in the more immediate neighborhood. I looked for some explosion of violence, for a screaming volley of oaths, for an hysteric burst of tears, perhaps for a missile of more questionable character than an epithet aimed at the head and shoulders projecting opposite. "At any rate," I thought, "their tongues will soon run down; for it is not in human nature that such a flow of scalding rhetoric can be kept up very long." But I stood waiting until I was tired, and with *labitur et labetur* on my lips, I left them pursuing the even tenor, or treble of their way in a duet which seemed as if it might go on until nightfall.

THE ONE-HOSS SHAY.

In 1880 or 1881 Dr. Holmes was elected a member of the National Association of Carriage Builders, perhaps in reference to his famous poem, " The One-Hoss Shay," or " Parson Turell's Legacy." He wrote them the following note : —

GENTLEMEN, — I am sorry that I cannot slip over into the meeting at the Grand Pacific Hotel in Chicago next Thursday evening ; but the stride would be a long one, and the only vehicle I was ever concerned in building went to pieces one day very suddenly. Besides, I am just now working in harness as a lecturer, and if I should bolt or run away I do not know what would become of the college vehicle to which I am attached. I must therefore content myself with wishing the company a good time, everybody happy, and not one sulky. Yours very truly,

O. W. HOLMES.

Appendix I.

THE CHORUS OF THE PALANQUIN BEARERS;
OR,
Dr. Palmer's Description of his Transit through
Cossitollah Street in Calcutta.

"What is this?   A close *palkee*, with a passenger; the bearers, with elbows sharply crooked, and calves all varicose, trotting to a monotonous, jerking ditty, which the *sirdar*, or leader, is impudently improvising, to the refrain of Putterum ('Easy now!'), at the expense of their fare's *amour-propre.*

'Out of the way there!
Putterum.
This is a Rajah!
Putterum.
Very small Rajah!
Putterum.
Sixpenny Rajah!
Putterum.
Holes in his elbows!
Putterum.
Capitan Slipshod!
Putterum.
Son of a sea-cook!
Putterum.
Hush! he will beat us!
Putterum.

Hush ! he will kick us !
Putterum.
Kick us and curse us !
Putterum.
Not he, the greenhorn !
Putterum.
Don't understand us !
Putterum.
Don't know the lingo !
Putterum.
Let's shake the palkee !
Putterum.
Rattle the pig's bones !
Putterum.
Set down the palkee !
Putterum.
Call him a great lord !
Putterum.
Ask him for buksheesh
Putterum.' ”

And so they do in this wise : —

" ' *Buksheesh do, Sahib ! buksheesh do !* O favorite slave of the Lord ! O tender shepherd of the poor ! O sublime and beautiful Being. . . . Bestow upon thy abject and self-despising slave wherewithal to commemorate the golden hour when, by a blessed dispensation, he was permitted to lay his trembling forehead against thy victorious feet.' ”

An explosion of wrath and threats bursting forth from the *palkee*, they suddenly change their minds and their tune, and as they go along chant in this style : —

   "'*Jeldie jou, jeldie!*
   (Trot up smartly!)
     Putterum.
   Carry him softly!
     Putterum.
   Swiftly and smoothly!
     Putterum.
   He is a Rajah!
     Putterum.
   Rich little Rajah!
     Putterum.
   Fierce little Rajah!
     Putterum.
   See how his eyes flash!
     Putterum.
   Hear how his voice roars!
     Putterum.
   He is a Tippoo!
     Putterum.
   Capitan Tippoo!
     Putterum.
   Tremble before him!
     Putterum.
   Serve him and please him!
     Putterum.
   Please him and serve him!
     Putterum.
   He will reward us!
     Putterum.
   He will protect us!
     Putterum.
   He will enrich us!
     Putterum.
   Charity, Lârd Sa'b!
     Putterum.
   Out of the way there!
     Putterum.
   Way for the great . . .
     Putterum.

Rajah of ten crores !
          Putter . . .
. . . Ten crores !
          Putter . . .
Rajah . . . .
               Put . . .
. . . Lârd . . . .
          Putter . . .
. . . . . . Sa'b !
          . . . . *rum.*'

" And so they have turned down Flag Street."

          Atlantic Monthly, January, 1858.

Appendix II.

Bibliography.

Published Works to Date, including Contributions to Periodical Literature.   With Notes.

Poetical Illustrations of the Athenæum Gallery of Paintings.   [Joint Author.]   Boston : True & Greene.   1827.

This little volume consists of poems, chiefly satirical, written by John Osborne Sargent, Park Benjamin, and Holmes.

The Harbinger : A May Gift, dedicated to the ladies who have so kindly aided the New England Institution for the Blind.   [Joint Editor.] Boston : Carter, Hendee, & Co.   1833.   12mo, pp. 96.

A collection of poems edited by Holmes and John Osborne Sargent.

Poems.   Boston : Otis, Broaders, & Co.   1836.

The first collected edition.

Boylston Prize Dissertations for the years 1836 and 1837.   Boston : Charles C. Little & James Brown.   1838.

Dedicated to Pierre Cha. Alex. Louis, Doctor of Medicine of the faculties of Paris and St. Petersburg.   The dissertations are three in number : (1) On Indigenous Intermittent Fever in New England.   (2) On Neuralgia.   (3) On Direct Exploration.

Marshall Hall's Principles of the Theory and Practice of Medicine. First American edition, revised and enlarged by Jacob Bigelow and O. W. Holmes. [Joint Editor.] Boston. 1839.

Homœopathy and its Kindred Delusions: Two Lectures delivered before the Boston Society for the Diffusion of Useful Knowledge. Boston: William D. Ticknor. 1842.

The Position and Prospects of the Medical Student. An Address delivered before the Boylston Medical Society of Harvard University, January 12, 1844. Boston: John Putnam, Printer. 1844.

Urania: A Rhymed Lesson. Pronounced before the Mercantile Library Association. Boston. 1846. 8vo.

Report of the Committee on Medical Literature. Published in Transactions of the American Medical Association, Volume I. 1847.

An Introductory Lecture, delivered at the Massachusetts Medical College, November 3, 1847. Boston: William D. Ticknor & Co. 1847.

See *Boston Medical and Surgical Journal*, xxxviii., 384 and 408.

Astraea: The Balance of Illusions. A Poem delivered before the Phi Beta Kappa Society of

Yale College, August 14, 1850.   Boston : Ticknor, Reed, & Fields.   1850.

A slender volume bound in boards and salmon-colored paper.

Poem, delivered at the dedication of the Pittsfield Cemetery, September 9, 1850.

The Benefactors of the Medical School of Harvard University; with a biographical sketch of the late Dr. George Parkman.   An Introductory Lecture delivered at the Massachusetts Medical College, November 7, 1850.   Boston : Ticknor, Reed, & Fields.   1850.

The Contagiousness of Puerperal Fever.   Read in 1843 before the Boston Society for Medical Improvement.   Reprinted from *New England Quarterly Journal of Medicine and Surgery.* Boston.   1855.

Oration delivered before the New England Society in the city of New York, at their Semi-Centennial Anniversary, December 22, 1855.   New York : Wm. C. Bryant & Co.

Published in the Society's Report of the Semi-Centennial Celebration, New York, 1856.

The Autocrat of the Breakfast-Table.   Every Man his own Boswell.   Boston : Ticknor & Fields. 1858.

The first octavo edition had illustrations.   The second — published in 1883 — is furnished with a new preface and notes by Dr. Holmes.

Valedictory Address to the Medical Graduates of Harvard University, March 10, 1858. Boston: David Clapp, 184 Washington Street. 1858.

Also published in the *Boston Medical and Surgical Journal*, lviii, 149-159.

The Professor at the Breakfast-Table ; with the story of Iris. Boston: Ticknor & Fields. 1859.

Currents and Counter-Currents in Medical Science : An Address delivered before the Massachusetts Medical Society at the annual meeting, May 30, 1860. Boston: Ticknor & Fields. 1860.

Vive la France ! Poem read by Dr. Holmes at the dinner given to H. I. H. the Prince Napoleon, September 25, 1861. Cambridge : Privately printed. 1861.

Printed along with the address of Edward Everett, given on the same occasion, in a slender, cream-colored libret

Elsie Venner: A Romance of Destiny. Boston : Ticknor & Fields. 1861.

Songs in Many Keys. Boston : Ticknor & Fields. 1861.

Dedicated to the poet's mother.

Border Lines of Knowledge in some Provinces of Medical Science. An Introductory Lecture delivered before the Medical Class of Harvard

University, November 6, 1861.   Boston: Ticknor & Fields.   1862.

A class lecture which treats of the work of Chemistry and the
Microscope in medicine and in physiology, accompanied by practical
remarks addressed to the students.

Edward Stafford's Medical Directions written for
Governor Winthrop in 1643, with Notes by
O. W. Holmes. [Annotator.] Boston. 1862.

Oration delivered before the City Authorities of
Boston, on the Fourth of July, 1863.   Boston:
Ticknor & Fields.   1863.

Reprinted in Philadelphia in 1863 for gratuitous distribution.
Also republished in Holmes' "Soundings from the Atlantic."

Soundings from the Atlantic.   Boston: Ticknor
& Fields.   1863.

Dedicated to Jacob Bigelow.

Teaching from the Chair and at the Bedside. An
Introductory Lecture delivered before the Medical Class of Harvard University, November 6,
1867.   Boston: David Clapp & Son.   1867.

The Guardian Angel.   Boston: Ticknor & Fields.
1867.

Dedicated to James T. Fields.

Atlantic Almanac for 1868. [Joint Editor with
Donald G. Mitchell.] Boston: Ticknor &
Fields, Office of the *Atlantic Monthly*.   1868.

This annual contains by Holmes "The Seasons" (1868, p. 2);
and "Talk concerning the Human Body and its Management"
(1869, p. 47).

The Medical Profession in Massachusetts. A Lecture read at the Lowell Institute, January 29, 1869.

Published by the Massachusetts Historical Society in 1869, in a volume entitled "Lectures delivered in a Course before the Lowell Institute, in Boston, by Members of the Massachusetts Historical Society, on Subjects Relating to the Early History of Massachusetts."

Valedictory Address, delivered to the Graduating Class of the Bellevue Hospital College, March 2, 1871. New York. 1871.

Reprinted from the *New York Medical Journal*, April, 1871.

Mechanism in Thought and Morals. An Address delivered before the Phi Beta Kappa Society of Harvard University, June 29, 1870, with Notes and Afterthoughts. Boston: Jas. R. Osgood & Co. 1871.

The Claims of Dentistry. An Address delivered at the Commencement Exercises of the Dental Department in Harvard University, February 14, 1872. Boston: Printed by Rand, Avery, & Co. 1872.

The Poet at the Breakfast-Table. Boston: James R. Osgood & Co. 1873.

Professor Jeffries Wyman. A Memorial Outline reprinted from the *Atlantic Monthly* for November, 1874. Boston and Cambridge. 1874.

Songs of Many Seasons. 1862–1874. Boston: James R. Osgood & Co. 1874.

An Address delivered at the Annual Meeting of the Boston Microscopical Society. Reprinted from *Boston Medical and Surgical Journal*, May 24, 1877. Cambridge: The Riverside Press. 1877.

Visions: A Study of False Sight (Pseudopia). By Edward Hammond Clarke, M.D. With an Introduction and Memorial Sketch by Oliver Wendell Holmes, M.D. [Editor.] Boston: Houghton, Osgood, & Co. 1878.

The School-Boy. Illustrated. Boston: Houghton, Osgood, & Co. 1878.

John Lothrop Motley. A Memoir. Boston: Houghton, Osgood, & Co. 1878.

The Iron Gate, and Other Poems. Boston: Houghton, Mifflin, & Co. 1880.

Address delivered at the Dedication of the Hall of the Boston Medical Library Association, 19 Boylston Place, on December 3, 1878. Cambridge: The Riverside Press. 1881.

Address on Emerson. Published in the Massachusetts Historical Society's "Tribute to Longfellow and Emerson." (Portraits.) Boston: A. Williams & Co. 1882.

CONTRIBUTIONS TO PERIODICAL LITERATURE.

THE ATLANTIC MONTHLY.

NOTE. — Poems are marked with an *, and prose articles not elsewhere reprinted with a †.

The Autocrat of the Breakfast-Table, Vols. I. and II. (1857); † Homœopathic Domestic Physician, I. 250 (1857); † Agassiz's Natural History, I. 320 (1858); † Parthenia (Lee), I. 509 (1858); A Visit to Autocrat's Landlady, II. 738 (1858); * The Last Look, II. 749 (1858); † Brief Expositions of Rational Medicine, II. 763 (1858); † The Autocrat gives a Breakfast to the Public, II. 889 (1858); † Mothers and Infants, Nurses and Nursing, III. 645 (1858); The Professor at the Breakfast-Table, III. and IV. (1859); The Stereoscope and the Stereograph, III. 738 (1859); † Love (Michelet), IV. 391 (1859); † The Undergraduate, V. 382 (1860); The Professor's Story, V. and VI. (1860); A Visit to the Asylum for Aged and Decayed Punsters, VII. 113 (1861); * Brother Jonathan's Lament for Sister Caroline, VII. 613 (1861); * Army Hymn, VII. 757 (1861); Sun Painting and Sun Sculpture, VIII. 13 (1861); * Parting Hymn, VIII. 235 (1861); Bread and the Newspaper, VIII. 346 (1861); † The Wormwood Cordial of History, VIII. 507 (1861); * The Flower of Liberty, VIII. 550 (1861);

* Union and Liberty, VIII. 756 (1861); * Voyage of the Good Ship Union, IX. 398 (1862); * The Poet to his Readers, X. 118 (1862); My Hunt after the Captain, X. 738 (1862); * " Choose ye this Day whom ye will Serve," XI. 288 (1863); The Human Wheel, its Spokes and Felloes, XI. 567 (1863); Doings of the Sunbeam, XII. 1 (1863); The Great Instrument, XII. 637 (1863); † The Minister Plenipotentiary, XIII. 106 (1864); * The Last Charge, XIII. 244 (1864); * Our Classmate, XIII. 329 (1864); † Our Progressive Independence, XIII. 497 (1864); * Shakespeare, XIII. 762 (1864); † Hawthorne, XIV. 98 (1864); * In Memory of J. W.—R. W., XIV. 115 (1864); * Bryant's Seventieth Birthday, XIV. 738 (1864); * God save the Flag, XV. 115 (1865); * Our Oldest Friend, XV. 340 (1865); * Our First Citizen, XV. 462 (1865); † Our Battle Laureate, XV. 589 (1865); * No Time like the Old Time, XVI. 398 (1865); * A Farewell to Agassiz, XVI. 584 (1865); * My Annual, XVII. 395 (1866); The Guardian Angel, XIX. and XX. (1867); * All Here, 1829–1867, XIX. 323 (1867); * Chanson without Music, XX. 543 (1867); * Once More, XXI. 430 (1868); * Bill and Joe, XXII. 313 (1868; † Cinders from the Ashes, XXIII. 115 (1869); * Bonaparte, XXIV. 637 (1869); * Nearing the Snow-Line, XXV. 86 (1870); * Even-Song, XXV. 349 (1870); * Dorothy Q., XXVII. 120 (1871); † Life of Major John André,

XXVIII. 121 (1871); The Poet at the Breakfast-Table, Vols. XXIX. and XXX. (1872); * After the Fire, XXXI. 96 (1872); * The Fountain of Youth, XXXII. 209 (1873); * A Poem served to Order, XXXII. 296 (1873); † Sex in Education (Dr. Clarke), XXXII. 737 (1873); * An Old Year Song, XXXIII. 101 (1874); * A Ballad of the Boston Tea-Party, XXXIII. 219 (1874); Professor Jeffries Wyman, XXXIV. 611 (1874); † The Americanized European, XXXV. 75 (1875); † Crime and Automatism, XXXV. 466 (1875); * Old Cambridge, XXXVI. 237 (1876); † Exotics, XXXVI. 356 (1876); * A Familiar Letter (to several correspondents), XXXVII. 103 (1876); * "Ad Amicos," 1829–1876, XXXVII. 314 (1876); * A Memorial Tribute (to Samuel G. Howe), XXXVII. 464 (1876); * How the Old Horse won the Bet, XXXVIII. 44 (1876); * The First Fan, XXXIX. 659 (1877); * How Not to Settle It, XXXIX. 257 (1877); * My Aviary, XLI. 122 (1878); * The Silent Melody, XLII. 335 (1878); * Vestigia Quinque Retrorsum, XLIV. 238 (1879); * The Coming Era, XLV. 84 (1880); * The Archbishop and Gil Blas, XLVI. 205 (1880); * Benjamin Peirce, XLVI. 824 (1880); * Boston to Florence, XLVII. 412 (1881); * Post-Prandial : Phi Beta Kappa, 1881, XLVIII. 365 (1881); * Our Dead Singer, XLIX. 721 (1882); * Before the Curfew, XLIX. 386 (1882); * At the Summit, L. 164 (1882); † An

After-Breakfast Talk, LI. 65 (1883) ; * Loving-Cup Song, LI. 349 (1883).

BUCKINGHAM'S NEW ENGLAND MAGAZINE.

The volumes for 1831, 1832, and 1833 contain contributions by Holmes as follows : Vol. I. (1831), "To an Insect " ; "A Week of Frailty " (describes a little street flirtation) ; " My Aunt " (poem) ; " The Autocrat of the Breakfast-Table (I.). — Vol. II. (1832) contains : " Old Books " (a bit of sentimental . bibliomania) ; " The Autocrat of the Breakfast-Table " (II.) ; " The Destroyers " (poem) ; " The Début."— Vol. III. (1833) contains, in a humorous paper by the editors which is styled " Report of the Editorial Department," a poetical production by Holmes, headed " A New Year's Address."

THE NORTH AMERICAN REVIEW.

The " Mechanism of Vital Actions " was published in the *North American Review* for July, 1857 ; the " Allston Exhibition " of paintings in the same for April, 1840 ; and " The Pulpit and the Pew " in the same for February, 1881.

THE INTERNATIONAL REVIEW.

The essay on " Jonathan Edwards " appeared in the *International Review*, Vol. IX. p. 1 (1880). Edwin Arnold's " Light of Asia " is reviewed in the same for October, 1879.

NEW ENGLAND QUARTERLY JOURNAL OF MEDICINE
AND SURGERY.

Dr. Holmes' "Contagiousness of Puerperal
Fever" was first published in the *New England
Quarterly Journal of Medicine and Surgery*, 1843,
edited by Drs. Charles E. Ware and Samuel Parkman : only one volume of the periodical was published.

PROCEEDINGS OF THE AMERICAN ACADEMY.

The Proceedings of the American Academy of
Arts and Sciences contains two communications
from Dr. Holmes. Vol. II., pp. 326–332, has a
paper "On the Use of Direct Light in Microscopical Researches," and a model by him of a
newly-invented horizontal microscopical apparatus
is figured. In Vol. IV., pp. 373–375, the term
" Reflex Vision " is proposed as a phrase proper
to certain original optical experiments, an account
of which is given.

BOSTON MEDICAL AND SURGICAL JOURNAL.

Microscopic Preparations, XLVIII. 337 ; Lines
written for the Eighth Anniversary of the American Medical Association, LII. 305 ; The Dental
Cosmos (review of), VIII. (new series), No. I. p.
99 ; Rip Van Winkle, M.D. : An After-Dinner
Prescription, taken by the Massachusetts Medical
Society at their meeting held May 25, 1870 ;

Address at Commencement Exercises of Dental
Department in Harvard University, February 14,
1877, IX. (new series), 9 ; The Physiology of Versification, XCII. 6–9 ; Poem on Joseph Warren,
XCII. 703 ; Letter on Dr. J. B. S. Jackson,
XCV. 393–395 ; Letter to Dr. George E. Ellis,
CIV. No. 25, p. 593 ; Poem written for the Centennial Anniversary Dinner of the Massachusetts
Medical Society, June 8, 1881, CIV. No. 25, pp.
577–580 ; Speech on occasion of the Presenta-
tion of a Portrait of Dr. J. B. S. Jackson to the
Boston Medical Library Association, CIV. No.
24, pp. 560, 561.

THE KNICKERBOCKER MAGAZINE

Contains a few youthful articles by Holmes which
might perhaps be identified.

BIBLIOGRAPHICAL NOTES.

THE first edition of the poems was published in
1836, by Otis, Broaders & Co., Boston.   The first
English edition was published in 1845.   London:
O. Rich & Sons, 12 Red Lion Square.   In 1852
Routledge published one edition, and another in
1853.

"Elsie Venner" has been translated and
abridged (with notes) by E. D. Forgues, in the

Revue des Deux Mondes for June 15 and July 1,
1861. The poem "There's no Time like the Old
Time " has been translated by Karl Knortz and
published in his "Amerikanische Gedichte der
Neuzeit." Leipsic. 1882.

A portion of the manuscript of "The Voyage
of the Good Ship Union " (poem) may be seen in
a glass case in the engraving-room of the Harvard
College Library.

The " Story of Iris " (from "The Professor at
the Breakfast-Table ") has been published in a
separate form in Vol. XXX. of the Vest-Pocket
Series of Modern Classics.

A volume of "Holmes Leaflets " has been
edited by Josephine E. Hodgson.

Holmes' "Army Hymn " was composed for
solo and chorus by Dresel, on the occasion of
the Beethoven Festival in Music Hall, March 1,
1856.

For articles in " The Atlantic Almanac," see the
present Bibliography (1868).

The manuscript of the poem, " Bonaparte, August 15, 1769 — Humboldt, September 14, 1769,"
may be seen in the Boston Public Library.

The poem entitled " Grandmother's Story of the
Bunker Hill Battle as she saw it from the Belfry,"
was originally printed in a volume entitled " Memorial. Bunker Hill, June 17, 1775–1875, with
illustrations by Harris M. Stevenson." Boston :
James R. Osgood & Co. 1875. A curiosity in

the typographical art is a folio copy of the above poem printed in mammoth type, — the lines being a foot across the page, — and to be seen at the Boston Public Library. It was privately printed, and only six copies were struck off. The one in the Public Library has written on it in pencil the words, "For old eyes." In a remarkable volume of autographic material on the battles of Lexington, Concord, and Bunker Hill, which has been made by Judge Mellen Chamberlain, Librarian of the Boston Public Library, may be seen an entire manuscript copy of the just-mentioned poem.

Dr. Holmes furnished an additional stanza (the fifth) for Francis Scott Key's "Star-Spangled Banner : Song and Chorus."

The "Visit to the Asylum for Aged and Decayed Punsters" (from "Soundings from the Atlantic") may be found in Vol. V. of Rossiter Johnson's "Little Classics."

The Autocrat has two articles in "The Harvard Book" (Cambridge : Welch, Bigelow, & Co. 1875), namely, "The Medical School," Vol. I., and "The Holmes Estate," Vol. II.

As a member of the Massachusetts Historical Society he has made various speeches and communicated various papers which are printed in the Proceedings of the Society and may be sought in the indexes to the same.

In Vol. III. of "The Boston Book" (1841)

was published Holmes' poem, " Departed Days,"
and his " Morning Visit."

Dr. Holmes' Farewell Lecture before the students of the Harvard Medical School is published
in the *Boston Medical and Surgical Journal* for
December 7, 1882; also in separate form by A.
Williams & Co., Boston.

In 1852 he delivered a course of lectures on
" The English Poets of the Nineteenth Century "
(still unpublished).

In November, 1864, he gave a lecture in Cambridge, Massachusetts, before the Dowse Institute,
entitled " New England's Master-Key."

In The Token and Atlantic Souvenir (edited by
S. G. Goodrich, Boston, 1838) will be found
Holmes' poem, " The Only Daughter." It accompanies an engraving by J. Andrews, from a painting by G. S. Newton. " The only daughter is represented as an old-fashioned-looking child, with
short hair and side-combs, enormous puffed sleeves
to her dress, which is cut low in the neck and over
which is tied a black silk apron with pockets,
while for ornament she wears a long string of
beads which goes twice around her neck, and is
tucked in her belt."

The following poems have been set to music:
Angel of Peace (Qt.), M. Keller; Army Hymn
(for Solo and Chorus), Dresel; Evening Thought,
Y. Van Antwerp; Hymn of Peace (Qt.), M. Keller; Song of a Clerk, A. J. Goodrich; There's no

Time like the Old Time (Song and Chorus), A. B. Hutchinson ; Welcome to the Nations (Qt.), M. Keller.

Dr. Holmes' medical lectures have occasionally been reprinted in English journals, such as the London *Lancet*.

INDEX.